*The Secret Book Club*

# Main Street

## The Secret Book Club

# Ann M. Martin

## SCHOLASTIC INC.

NEW YORK ◇ TORONTO ◇ LONDON ◇ AUCKLAND ◇ SYDNEY
MEXICO CITY ◇ NEW DELHI ◇ HONG KONG ◇ BUENOS AIRES

*For the members of my book club:*
*Amy, Gaela, Jamey, Debi, Nell, Ann, and Anne*

ISBN-13: 978-0-439-86883-9
ISBN-10: 0-439-86883-1

Illustrations by Dan Andreason

12 11 10 9 8 7 6 5 4 3 2 1          8 9 10 11 12 13/0

Printed in the U.S.A.                                    23

First printing, July 2008

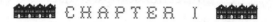

# CHAPTER I

# Book Club Summer

Flora Northrop sat on her front stoop and surveyed Aiken Avenue. Early morning was one of her favorite times of day, and an early summer morning was especially delicious. On this Friday in late June, Flora inhaled deeply and caught the scent of grass, of rose petals, and of something soft and sweet that eventually she realized was rain. It had rained the night before — the trees were vaguely drippy — and it looked like it would probably rain again later that day. Flora didn't care. She liked rain.

"Ruby!" called Min from the other side of the door. "Please get a move on. It's time to go."

Flora listened for her sister's response and heard nothing.

"Ruby Jane!" called Min a moment later, and Flora

thought her grandmother sounded just the teeniest bit impatient now. "Ruby?"

"*What? I'm com*ing!"

Min, who had opened the front door, now ducked back inside. "Ruby, I hope that what I just heard you say was, 'I'm on my way, Min dear.'"

Flora turned around, smiling. But when she caught sight of her sister's face, her smile disappeared. Ruby looked like a storm cloud.

"For corn's sake," said Min. "Ruby, what's the matter?"

"I don't want to go to the store," replied Ruby, an impressive whine to her voice. "Are we going to have to go *every* day this summer?"

Min turned a gaze on her granddaughter that said "What do *you* think?" as plainly as if she had used words.

"All right. I know we won't be going every *single* day," said Ruby huffily. "I just don't want to go today. It's too early. I wanted to sleep late. Isn't that what summer vacation is for?"

"If you're a sloth," said Min.

Flora got to her feet. "Come on, Ruby. Hey, I know what will make you happy. I saw the baby phoebes when I woke up this morning."

"The babies? The phoebe had her babies?" Ruby brightened, and Min shot Flora a grateful glance.

"Yup," replied Flora.

Three pairs of eyes looked up to the window box outside Flora's room. In it was a mossy nest built by a shy phoebe.

"Did all the eggs hatch?" asked Ruby.

"All three," said Flora.

"Just like last year," said Ruby, and she skipped along the path to the sidewalk while Min locked the door of the Row House.

Just like last year, thought Flora with amazement. It was hard to believe that she and her sister had lived in Camden Falls long enough to say that. But they were, in fact, beginning their second year in their new home.

Flora and Min caught up with Ruby and turned right when they reached the sidewalk.

"Malone!" announced Ruby as she passed the Malones' front walk. Her mood was brightening. "Willet!" she called as she passed the next walk. And finally, "Morris!"

Flora, Ruby, and Min lived in the Row Houses, the only building of its kind in Camden Falls, Massachusetts — eight attached homes, nearly identical, built well over a hundred years earlier. Mindy Read's, the fourth from the left, was the house in which she had grown up, the house in which she and her husband had raised their two daughters, and now the house in which she was raising Flora and Ruby, her granddaughters.

Ruby ran ahead of Min and Flora, reached Dodds Lane, and doubled back. "Come on, slowpokes," she said. Then, "Hey, Min, I need new tap shoes. My old ones are squeezing my toes, and I'll be starting Turbo Tappers in August. I can't have tight shoes then."

"We'll order them from Hulit's," said Min. "Remind me at lunchtime. We'll go to the store and pay a visit to Mrs. Hulit."

Flora still marveled at the fact that Min knew every single shopkeeper on Main Street. But then, Min had owned Needle and Thread for many, many years. And the people who worked in the stores, like the people who lived in the Row Houses, were a close community.

Flora, Ruby, and Min walked along Dodds Lane for a block, then turned right on Main Street. Ruby took her grandmother's hand. "Min?" she said. "Do you think I'm going to be bored this summer?"

"Sweetie, when a person has as many interests as you do," Min answered, "or as many as Flora does," she added hastily, "I should think it would be hard for her to be bored."

"Yes," said Ruby, "but this spring I was in the play *and* I had dance classes *and* chorus rehearsals —"

"Not to mention school," said Min.

"Yeah, and school. Now I don't have anything to do until Turbo Tappers starts. That's over a month away."

Min sighed. "Ruby —" But she was interrupted by Flora, who was stooping in the doorway of Needle and Thread.

"Hey!" Flora exclaimed.

"What?" cried Ruby. "What is it, Flora?"

"Look!" Flora straightened up and held out four mailing envelopes for her sister's inspection. "They have our names on them. I mean, one has my name, one has yours, one has Olivia's, and one has Nikki's. They were just sitting here stacked up by the door. I wonder where they came from."

"The mailman," said Ruby.

Flora gave her sister a withering look. "Mail isn't delivered in the middle of the night. Plus, these don't have stamps on them. They don't even have addresses on them. Or our last names!"

Ruby reached for her package and hefted it on the palm of one hand. "Not too heavy," she said.

Flora appealed to her grandmother. "Min, look. Who do you think these came from?"

Min busied herself searching through her giant pocketbook for the keys to the store. Flora imagined the jumble that was inside that purse: Life Savers and Kleenex and loose change, a mirror, a comb, a pen, Min's reading glasses, earrings, buttons, notes, her bulging wallet, and several key rings.

"Ah, here we go," said Min, inserting a key into the

lock on the door. "Oh. No. Wrong one." She began the search through her purse again.

"Min!" said Flora urgently. "Isn't this strange?"

At that moment, Min thrust the door open.

"I'm going to look in my package right now," said Ruby.

"No," said Flora. "Don't you think we should wait until Nikki and Olivia are here so we can open them together?"

Ruby gasped suddenly. "What if they're from a psycho?" she cried, and dropped the package to the floor.

"They're not from a psycho." Flora picked up the envelope and handed it back to her sister. "Min wouldn't let us open something from a psycho. Come on. Let's call Olivia and Nikki."

"It's a bit early for that," said Min, depositing the keys and her purse on the counter by the cash register. "You'd better wait until nine."

"Waiting," said Flora, "is not Ruby's strong point."

"No. But I have many other strong points," said Ruby with great dignity.

Flora sat on one of the couches at the front of the store, where later in the day customers would drop in for a friendly chat-and-stitch. She opened a sewing magazine but kept one eye on her watch. The moment it read exactly nine o'clock, she bolted for the telephone and called Olivia Walter.

"Olivia!" Flora exclaimed. "The weirdest thing

happened!" She told her about the envelopes. "So you have to come to the store right away!" She placed a similar call to Nikki Sherman, then returned to the couch and her magazine.

"How can you sit there reading like nothing happened?" asked Ruby after a few moments. She looked at her own watch.

Flora shrugged. "I just can."

"Well, when are they going to get here?"

"As soon as possible."

"When is that?"

Flora paused and was trying to formulate a reasonable answer when Min said, "Ruby, please go give Gigi a hand with those boxes in the back."

Gigi, who was Olivia's grandmother and Min's business partner, had arrived while Flora was on the phone with Nikki. Now she was in the back of the store, struggling with several cartons of new supplies that had been delivered the afternoon before. Ruby joined her, glad for a job.

Flora, relishing the peace that would probably last only a few minutes until the first customer arrived, laid down the magazine and gazed out at Main Street. The year since she and Ruby had moved to Camden Falls seemed to her both very long and very short. There had been days that had dragged by, days when Flora could think of nothing but her parents and the accident, days that had each felt as long as a whole year. But in between those bad days, so much had happened that sometimes Flora marveled that it had all taken place in *just* a year.

Flora remembered the June afternoon when she and Ruby had made their move to Camden Falls, the day the U-Haul had been packed up and Min had driven them, along with Daisy Dear (her dog) and King Comma (Flora and Ruby's cat) from their old home, hours away, to the Row Houses on Aiken Avenue. Min had turned onto Main Street, the U-Haul clanking along behind her car, and Flora had passed Time and Again, Frank's Beans, Heaven, Needle and Thread, the library, College Pizza, and all the sights that were now as familiar to Flora as old friends. But on that ride, Flora had barely noticed Main Street; her mind was only on what she had left behind — the house in which she and Ruby had been born, her school, her best friend, and the memories of her parents, who had died in the accident on an icy road five months earlier.

After the accident, busy Min (whose name was short both for Mindy and for "in a minute," something she used to say all the time to her granddaughters) had arrived, bustling and businesslike, and helped Flora and Ruby to reassemble the pieces of their lives. Flora had been ten then and Ruby eight, and while they had been relieved and grateful for Min's efficient presence, they still hadn't wanted to move to Camden Falls.

And now they had been in Camden Falls for a year, Flora reflected as she watched old Mrs. Grindle unlock the door to Stuff 'n' Nonsense across the street, and another summer was beginning. She wondered if this summer would be as eventful as the previous one. She hoped so, for Ruby's sake. Flora didn't mind spending time with Min and Gigi at Needle and Thread, but Ruby needed activities. Min *had* said that maybe this summer the girls could be more independent. Flora was contemplating what, exactly, that might mean when she saw Olivia Walter sprinting along Main Street. She bounced through the door and slid onto the couch next to Flora.

"Where are they?" Olivia asked breathlessly.

Flora pointed to the coffee table.

Olivia made a grab for her package. "Huh," she said. "Weird."

"Here's Nikki," Flora announced as Nikki chained her bicycle to a rack on the sidewalk. Then Flora called to Ruby, "Everyone's here."

Moments later, the girls had crowded onto the couch, each holding her envelope. They sat squished together in a row — Nikki, her face pale, freckles scattered across her nose, brown hair tousled; Olivia, wild dark hair in a cloud around her face; and Flora and Ruby, with wide-set eyes and round faces, Flora's framed by brown hair that she resisted cutting, and Ruby's by blond hair that she wished were curlier.

"Ready?" said Olivia. "One, two . . . three!"

In a flash, the envelopes were ripped open. From each was withdrawn two paperback books and a letter.

"*The Saturdays*, by Elizabeth Enright, and *Mrs. Frisby and the Rats of NIMH*, by Robert O'Brien," said Flora, holding one book in each hand. "Did we all get the same books?"

"Yup," said the others.

"Let's see what the letter says."

"Do you suppose we all got the same letter, too?" asked Ruby.

"Probably," said Flora.

"I'll read mine aloud then," said Nikki. She drew in a breath. "'Welcome!'" she began. "'You and your friends have been chosen — just the four of you — to be members of a secret summer book club.'"

"Just the four of us," said Olivia thoughtfully. "Someone knows us well."

"'Every few weeks,'" Nikki continued, "'a package will arrive containing a new book. I hope you will have fun reading each book together and talking about it. The book will be accompanied by a letter, such as this one, that will include activities, things to discuss, and some instructions to follow.'"

"Ooh, mysterious," said Ruby.

"'*The Saturdays*,'" Nikki went on, "'is a bonus book. Future selections will contain one book only. Read

*The Saturdays* first. Like the Melendys, you will be having lots of Saturday adventures this summer.'"

"Who are the Melendys?" asked Olivia.

"They must be characters in *The Saturdays*," Flora replied.

"Saturday adventures," said Ruby dreamily. "I like the sound of that."

"Ahem," said Nikki. "'Then read *Mrs. Frisby and the Rats of NIMH*. When each of you has finished *Mrs. Frisby*, please do the following: First discuss the story.' Then there's a whole list of things to talk about," said Nikki.

"But look what comes next," said Flora, running her finger down her own letter. "Read what it says under 'Activity.'"

"'For your first Saturday adventure, think up and carry out a fun project that will help make Camden Falls a "greener" place,'" said Nikki.

Olivia looked puzzled. "I guess we'll know what that means after we finish the book."

"Hey!" exclaimed Nikki. "Listen to the end of the letter. 'On the day of your final Saturday adventure, the person behind the book club will be revealed. Happy reading!' And the letter just ends that way. It isn't signed or anything."

Ruby scanned her letter again. "Well . . . well . . ."

"Hey, Ruby's speechless!" crowed Olivia.

Flora giggled. "But really — who sent these?"

"Min?" suggested Ruby. "Gigi?"

Everyone turned to look at Min and Gigi, who were talking earnestly with a customer.

"Somehow I don't think so," said Flora.

"Let's not try to figure it out," said Nikki. "At least not right away. I like having a mystery."

Olivia frowned. "I can't help trying to figure it out. That's just how my brain works."

"Well, I'm going to start reading," said Flora.

"At least," said Ruby, "the summer isn't going to be boring after all."

# CHAPTER 2

# Sirens in the Night

Ruby felt that, of the group of friends consisting of Nikki, Olivia, Flora, and herself — Ruby Jane Northrop — she was more different from the rest of them than any of the others were. She knew that the other girls would not agree. For one thing, everyone is different. Min said so all the time. And of course each of the girls was unique. And *Flora* said there aren't degrees of uniqueness. You're either unique or you aren't. But Ruby didn't agree. She felt she was the most unique.

Olivia was different from the others because she was so smart — frighteningly smart, really. She had skipped a grade and could still master her schoolwork far more handily than any of her year-older classmates. Plus, she could read at the speed of light. Nikki was different because she lived way on the other side of

Camden Falls, while Flora and Ruby lived within inches of Olivia. Nikki's family had been in turmoil for years while her alcoholic parents tried to get their lives under control. Ruby could barely fathom such a thing. Flora was different because she was the shyest of the girls (even shyer than Nikki, which was saying a lot), and she possessed many solitary talents, such as her love of writing and her ability to sew and do needlework as well as most adults.

And then there was Ruby. She was younger than the others, even younger than Olivia, and while in the fall the rest of the girls would begin seventh grade at Camden Falls Central High School, Ruby would remain behind at Camden Falls Elementary to start fifth grade, where, she already knew, she would not distinguish herself as a student, unlike the older girls, who frequently earned A's and won scholastic awards. Furthermore, there was the issue of Ruby's talents. Nikki, Olivia, and Flora each had talents, but they were of the less showy sort, such as Flora's needlework and Nikki's artwork and Olivia's tendency to win blue ribbons at science fairs. Ruby, on the other hand, possessed talents of great noise and flourish. She could sing. She could dance. She could act. And she did all three as frequently as possible in front of as many people as possible. She couldn't imagine what it felt like to be shy — although she had occasionally had to *act* shy in order to play a part realistically. So Ruby was quite confident that although each of the four friends was one of a kind, she was the most one of a kind.

She was thinking about this as she climbed into bed on the evening of the day on which the secret book club packages arrived. Yet another thing that set Ruby apart from her sister and Nikki and Olivia was her lack of interest in reading. Ruby was a good reader; there was no question of that. She could read and memorize scripts in a jiffy. And when asked to read aloud in school, her teachers always said she read with great expression, which apparently implied that her comprehension was good. But spend a perfectly good summer afternoon curled up reading? Or wake up early in the morning in order to read before it was time to get ready for school? That was not Ruby's style.

She glanced at *Mrs. Frisby and the Rats of NIMH* and *The Saturdays* sitting on her bedside table. *The Saturdays* was on top, since the girls were supposed to read it first. Ruby reached for it and settled back against her pillows, King Comma under the covers, resting warmly against her leg.

Ruby lifted the blanket and peered in at King. "It's, like, eighty degrees outside," she said to the cat. "How can you stand to be under there? You're going to melt."

King opened his eyes, yawned widely, and closed his eyes again.

Ruby looked at the cover of the book and then at an illustration inside that showed four kids she guessed were the Melendys.

"What an odd name," she said to King.

At last she turned to Chapter One and began to read. She read determinedly for four pages and decided the book was rather old-fashioned and that if not for the secret club, she probably wouldn't finish it. (This was another difference between her and Olivia, Nikki, and Flora. The older girls had started the book that morning — and loved it — and Olivia was already on Chapter Seven.) But Ruby persevered. After all, the letter had mentioned Saturday adventures, and the book was called *The Saturdays*. She was rewarded when, several pages later, Randy Melendy (who, despite her name, was a girl) came up with the idea of a club, which her brother Rush suggested calling the Independent Saturday Afternoon Adventure Club. Well, that was more interesting.

Ruby reached the end of Chapter One, returned the book to her table, switched off her reading light, and lay in the dark. Through her partly open door she could see that Flora's light was still on. She was probably sailing through *The Saturdays*. Ruby rolled onto her side and lay in the sticky night air. She listened to King's rumbly purr and to the singing of crickets. Her eyelids drooped.

When the sirens started, Ruby was dreaming that

King Comma had escaped from the Row House and was lost in a fierce rainstorm. Ruby could hear him yowling and howling.

"King!" she called in the dream. "King, I'm right here!"

The howling became more insistent and Ruby opened her eyes. That was when she realized that the noise was real, only it wasn't a cat's howl, it was the shriek of a fire engine — of several fire engines.

Ruby smelled smoke. She sat up, sniffing.

*Oooooo-OOOOOOO-oooooo.* The wail of the sirens rose and fell.

Ruby scrambled to her window and peered through the screen. She could see flames, and they weren't far away. A fire engine rushed along Dodds Lane and screeched around the corner, making a left onto Main Street. Another one followed it, and then another and another.

Ruby switched on her reading light and looked at her clock. Two-forty. She leaped from her bed, opened her door, and crashed into a bleary-eyed Flora in the hall.

"A fire on Main Street!" cried Ruby.

"I think it's Plaza Drugs!" said Flora.

"Min! Min!" called Ruby.

Min shuffled drowsily out of her bedroom, tying a robe around her ample waist. "Girls?"

"Fire!" exclaimed Ruby.

Min and Flora followed Ruby into her room, and they crowded around the window. In the distance, orange and yellow flames roared into the air.

"It's noisy. A fire is noisy," said Ruby in wonderment. She shivered.

"Don't you think it's Plaza Drugs?" Flora asked Min.

"Maybe. That's about the right spot."

"Can we go into town?" asked Ruby.

"*Now?*" exclaimed Min. "It's the middle of the night."

"But I want to see."

"Absolutely not. But I think I will just call the rescue squad and make sure the fire hasn't spread to the next block. We'll learn more tomorrow morning as soon as we get to the store. If not before," added Min, thinking of how quickly news spread in Camden Falls.

Min returned to her bed, but Flora and Ruby, shoulder to shoulder at Ruby's window, watched the activity (what little they could make out in the distance) until they felt dizzy with fatigue and Flora said she was falling asleep. She crossed the hall to her room, and Ruby finally joined King under the covers again.

Ruby had thought she might feel tired in the morning, but she was awake before her alarm went off, and was dressed and ready to leave for Needle and Thread while

Flora and Min were still sitting groggily in front of bowls of cereal at the kitchen table.

"Come *on*! Let's *go*!" said Ruby, standing impatiently by the front door.

"It takes an actual fire to get her up early on a summer morning," muttered Flora, and Min smiled.

"Well, I'm going to wait for you outside," said Ruby, and she stepped onto the front stoop and looked up and down the Row Houses, hoping for the sight of a neighbor who might have a tidbit of information.

The house on the far left belonged to the Fongs, a young couple, artists, who had recently had their first baby. Flora didn't expect to see them up at this hour, what with the nighttime feedings Min was always talking about. Next to the Fongs lived Robby Edwards and his family, and on the other side of Robby's house were Mr. Pennington's and then Olivia's. No one in that direction.

Ruby turned her head to the right. No one there, either. Oh, well. She sat on her stoop, then stood up again when she heard someone call her name.

"Ruby! Ruby! Did you hear? It was a big fire last night!"

Robby Edwards had emerged from his house and was running across the lawns.

Ruby stood up. "I know! I saw the fire engines."

"Me, too, Ruby! I like fire engines." Robby paused.

"But I don't like fire. I'm glad it wasn't Sincerely Yours that caught on fire. Or Needle and Thread. Or College Pizza. Or Dutch Haus." Robby Edwards, who was eighteen years old and had Down syndrome, had recently begun his first job working alongside Olivia's parents at Sincerely Yours, their new store on Main Street.

"What *did* catch fire, Robby? Do you know?" asked Ruby eagerly.

"Yes, I know. We heard on the radio this morning. It was the Marquis Diner."

Two thoughts crossed Ruby's mind at exactly the same time. One was, Why didn't I think to turn on the radio? The other was, What's the Marquis Diner?

"What's the Marquis Diner?" she asked Robby.

"It's next to Plaza Drugs. It's a new restaurant."

"Oh, *that* place. In between Plaza Drugs and Hulit's, right?"

"Right, Ruby."

Min and Flora hurried out the front door then, and Ruby and Robby chorused, "The Marquis Diner burned down!"

Flora frowned. "You don't have to sound so excited."

"But it *is* exciting," said Robby. "Well, I have to go get ready for work now. Bye."

"Bye, Robby," said Ruby and Flora.

"We'd better get a move on," said Min. "We're a little poky this morning."

"Not me!" cried Ruby, running ahead.

Min, Flora, and Ruby made their way down Aiken Avenue. By the time they reached the corner, they had stopped to speak with Dr. Malone, Mr. Willet, and Ruby's friend Lacey Morris, and had heard three different stories about the fire: It had started in Plaza Drugs and spread to the Marquis, and no one was hurt. It had started in the Marquis and spread to Hulit's, and one person had been injured. It had been contained in the Marquis, and a firefighter had been slightly injured.

Ruby thought of the flames she had seen the night before and remembered the sound of the sirens in the night. She pictured the fire engines whizzing along. Robby was right. This was exciting, the most exciting thing that had happened in town in ages. Still hurrying along in front of Min and Flora, Ruby reached Main Street, and instead of turning right to go to Needle and Thread, she turned left — and came to a standstill.

A small crowd of people stood outside the building that housed Plaza Drugs, the new diner, and Hulit's shoe store. The people were standing in the street, and Ruby saw that a section of Main Street had been closed off.

"Oh, no," said Min, putting her hand to her mouth as she and Flora joined Ruby.

Ruby's excitement vanished suddenly and a sick feeling crept into her stomach. She stared at the ruined building, the sidewalk in front of it blackened and wet. The windows of Plaza Drugs and Hulit's were broken and everything inside was covered in shards of glass but otherwise didn't look too bad. However, between the stores, the newly opened diner was destroyed. From where Ruby stood, she saw nothing inside but a gaping charred room, still dripping with water from the fire hoses. She slipped her hand in Min's.

"Oh, my," whispered Min.

Gigi joined them. "What a shame," she said, and Min nodded. "I heard that the drugstore and Hulit's can be repaired fairly easily — they'll only be closed for a few weeks — but that the people who bought the Marquis will have to start over from scratch."

Someone standing just behind Ruby said, "There they are now."

"Who?" asked someone else.

"The Nelsons. The owners of the Marquis."

Ruby stood on her tiptoes, saw nothing but shoulders, then squirmed through the crowd until she had a better view of the building. She saw a tired-looking man, a tired-looking woman, and two dazed children — a boy of about five and a girl about Ruby's own age — gathered around a police officer. The woman looked as though she'd been crying.

As Ruby stood staring, she was surprised to see Min and Gigi make their way to the Nelsons, hold out their hands, and introduce themselves. Then Min said, "Our store is just over there." She pointed down Main Street.

"Please come by later, all four of you," added Gigi. "We'll get the coffee started."

"That's — that's lovely of you," said Mrs. Nelson, sounding surprised.

"You're part of Camden Falls now," was Min's brisk reply.

Ruby, her earlier excitement completely drained from her body, followed Min, Gigi, and Flora meekly to the safe haven of Needle and Thread.

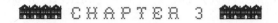 

# CHAPTER 3

# A Peek in the Windows

On a Friday night in Camden Falls, Massachusetts, population 14,767, some people are wherever they usually are in the evening, and others are not where one might expect to find them. On Friday nights, things and people get shuffled around a little. Come peek inside some of the homes in Camden Falls and find out who's where.

Darkness has not fallen yet, so there's time to take a walk through the still, hot air and stand outside a cottage surrounded by tidy gardens that, during the day, are abuzz with bees. In fact, later in the summer if you were to stand beneath the hydrangea in the front yard, you would find the entire bush humming loudly. This is Mary Woolsey's house, and Mary is at home, as she usually is. But this evening, instead of eating supper in her tiny kitchen, she's sitting contentedly in her garden, thinking of the afternoon she spent working at Needle and Thread. Her thoughts are interrupted when she sees a flash of bright blue zip through the murky air and light on a branch of the forsythia bush. She exclaims aloud, "Well, I never! An indigo bunting. What is an indigo bunting doing here?" She reaches for her binoculars to get a better view of this bird, which is most certainly not where it is supposed to be.

Leave Mary's and walk several blocks to a street that is unfamiliar to Flora and Ruby Northrop. Standing in front of a plain one-story house with about as much personality as a hen (a saying of Min's that Ruby thinks is supremely unfair to hens) is a weary family. The father looks ruefully at the FOR RENT sign sticking out of a clump of overgrown grass and says, "I guess we can take this down now." These are the Nelsons, and they are definitely not where they expected to be this Friday night, or any night at all once they had moved to Camden Falls. They had planned to live in the apartment over the diner, but the apartment had been ruined along with the diner, and they have scrambled to find a house to rent while the diner is being repaired.

"Can we afford this?" asks Hilary Nelson, who's ten.

"You shouldn't be worrying about things like that,"

replies her mother, putting her arm around Hilary's shoulders.

Hilary shrugs away from her mother. "You and Dad said that the insurance would pay for the repairs, but this is extra. How can we afford it?"

Hilary knows that her parents used up almost all of their money in order to leave Boston and start their own business here in this small town, something they'd been dreaming of doing for years.

Mr. Nelson sighs. "We're not sure we can," he says, and Hilary, looking at the shabby house, begins to cry.

"But we're going to give it the summer to see what happens," adds Mrs. Nelson. "We'll just have to start over again."

"We *already* started over again," says Hilary, "but this time we don't have anything to start over again *with*." She edges away from her little brother so he won't see her tears.

Mrs. Nelson pulls an unfamiliar key out of her pocket and inserts it in the lock on the front door of the house.

Darkness is falling now, but the air is sweet and the night is gentle, and it's a good time to take a walk in the countryside to the home of Nikki Sherman. On this Friday, Nikki and her little sister, Mae, are at home, but Nikki's brother is out, and her mother is in town having dinner with an old friend. This is so unusual that Nikki actually cannot remember another time when her mother met a friend for dinner. In the first place, the Shermans have little money for extras and luxuries. In the second place, Mrs. Sherman doesn't have any friends.

Well, thinks Nikki, that can't be true. Her mother must have had friends at some time in her life. But while she was living with Nikki's father, friendships were not encouraged. Now things are different. Nikki's father is gone, and the rest of the Shermans are far happier than they were when he was present.

"Nikki," says Mae, "something came in the mail for Tobias today. And I don't think it's a bill. It looks like a letter." This is also unusual. The Shermans don't get a lot of mail apart from bills and flyers. "I wish Tobias was at home," Mae continues. "I want to see what he got."

Nikki examines the envelope on the kitchen table. "Huh," she says. "The return address is for some college in Connecticut. Why would Tobias be getting a letter from a college?"

"Let's open it!" says Mae.

Nikki smiles. "Nope. Can't do that. This is Tobias's personal, private mail. He's the only one who can open it. And he's with his friends and won't be home until after you're in bed. Asleep."

"Oh, bullfrogs," says Mae.

Nikki smiles again. "Come on, let's take Paw-Paw out for one last walk, and then I'll read to you."

The Shermans' porch light winks on, and Nikki and Mae, hand in hand, step outside into the last of the light.

The moon is rising and the nighttime creatures have begun their chirping and calling. If you walk down the Shermans' rutted lane to the paved road now, a breeze will ruffle your hair. Head east back to Camden Falls. When you reach town, turn onto Main Street and stroll past the stores and businesses. Their windows are dark, except for the restaurants'. Walk by Needle and Thread, which looks asleep, College Pizza (Tobias is in there with his friends), and Dutch Haus, where Robby and his parents are sitting around a tippy table with ice-cream cones.

If you make a left after Dutch Haus and then a right, you'll find yourself on Aiken Avenue, and ahead of you will loom the Row Houses. In the first one, the one on the left end, are the four Morris children. They're giddy with excitement because their parents are out for the evening, and Margaret Malone, their baby-sitter, has just suggested that they play a game of Airhead. The children don't know what Airhead is, but if Margaret has invented it, then it's sure to be wonderful.

The house next to the Morrises', the Willets', is dark. Old Mr. Willet has driven out to Three Oaks to visit his wife. He looks forward to these visits, even though Mrs. Willet is no longer certain who he is. Sometimes she recognizes him as her husband, but sometimes she thinks he's her brother or, more often than not, just a strange man.

The Malones' house is dark, too. Dr. Malone and his daughters are scattered on this Friday night, although Margaret will return home as soon as Mr. and Mrs. Morris do.

Next to the Malones', Min's house is awash in light. In a room on the second floor, Flora has pulled out her mother's diary, the one she found nearly a year earlier when she moved into the room in which her mother grew up. "Ruby!" Flora calls. "Come look at Mom's diary with me!"

"No!" Ruby calls from across the hall. "I'm busy reading *The Saturdays*." This is not true. Ruby is not reading or doing anything at all. But she does not want to see her mother's diary.

Downstairs, Min sits in the living room with her old friend Mr. Pennington. They are smiling at each other and listening to the skreeking of the crickets through the open windows.

Next door is another dark house. Olivia and her family have gone to the movies. Mr. Pennington's house is dark, too (only Jacques, his aged dog, is at home, snoozing on the couch), and so is Robby's house. But at the last house, the one on the right end, pale light shines from the window of a second-floor room in which Mr. Fong is trying to soothe Grace into sleep. Light also shines from the window of the kitchen below, where Mrs. Fong is simultaneously making dinner and feeding two bouncy dogs. "Hush," she says softly to the dogs. "Hush or you'll wake the baby."

It's getting late now, but there's time to peek in one final window before Camden Falls starts to go to bed. Come away from Aiken Avenue and walk toward the elementary school to a fine house with a pool in the backyard. Many windows are lit in this house, and if you were to peek into the one at the west end of the second floor you would find Tanya Rhodes, a classmate of Flora, Olivia, and Nikki's. Tanya is planning a pool party and she is busily drawing up the guest list. Several names are already on the list, names of girls who were in her sixth-grade class with Mr. Donaldson. Tanya pauses, then adds Flora's name to the list, then Nikki's, and, finally, Olivia's. She puts her pen down, considers the names, and picks up the pen again.

She crosses Olivia Walter off the list.

# CHAPTER 4

# *Not Invited*

Olivia Walter was aware that some things about her —
actually, many things — had led her classmates to
decide she was weird. This was not fair. After all, was it
Olivia's fault that she had skipped a grade? No. It was
not. Her parents and teachers had made her do that.
Was it Olivia's fault that she had a late birthday, and
that while most of her friends and classmates had
already turned twelve, Olivia was still only ten? No. It
was not. Olivia had very much enjoyed the surprise
one-oh party her friends had given her the previous
fall, but it had done nothing to help her catch up with
the twelve-year-olds. Was it Olivia's fault that she was
small for her age and that she apparently could do
absolutely nothing to tame the mass of black curls that
bounced around her head like springs? No. It was not.
She couldn't help how she was born. Was it Olivia's

fault that what interested her most was not soccer or fashion or dances but birds of prey and weather conditions and chemical properties? Well, maybe that was Olivia's fault. Maybe this summer she could try to expand her interests a bit. But she couldn't just *make* herself interested in something that didn't actually interest her, could she?

Olivia was very grateful that she finally had friends, and that she truly did share interests with them, or at least with Flora and Nikki. Olivia and Ruby had little in common, except that (Olivia had recently realized with horror) she was actually slightly closer in age to Ruby than she was to the others. But Olivia, Flora, and Nikki shared a love of reading and of quieter pursuits. Furthermore, Nikki had set her sights on one day becoming a wildlife artist, which meant she spent a good deal of time studying the animals and insects she drew.

Olivia sighed. She had a feeling she and Nikki and Flora would never be popular kids, not like the older girls Olivia saw hanging around in front of the central school — the very school at which she would become a student in the fall.

Oh, well. Olivia was not going to ruin her summer by worrying about these things. On this cozy, rainy day, she and Flora were happily occupying one of the couches at the front of Needle and Thread. They were lying on their backs, Flora's head resting on one arm of the couch, Olivia's on the other, their feet just far enough from each other's faces so that neither was tempted to complain about any odors. Gigi and Min were helping customers; Mary Woolsey was working at her table in the back, pinning up the hems on all the dresses for a bridal party; and two women were busily paging through the catalogs of sewing patterns. A peaceful, rainy June afternoon.

Olivia and Flora were reading *Mrs. Frisby and the Rats of NIMH*, having already finished *The Saturdays*. Olivia was turning pages so fast that Flora was beginning to find it annoying, when the door to the store opened and in walked Nikki, holding an envelope in one hand and appearing puzzled.

She fanned the air with the envelope and said, "Look. Look at this."

"What is it?" asked Olivia, sitting up.

"We sure have been getting some interesting mail at our house lately," Nikki continued.

"What *is* it?" said Flora.

Nikki sat on the couch between her friends and pulled a card out of the envelope. "It's an invitation." Nikki paused. "To a pool party at Tanya's house. *Tanya's.*"

"Tanya *Rhodes*?" asked Olivia incredulously, and Nikki nodded.

"Wow," said Flora.

"It must be a joke," said Nikki.

Flora and Olivia crowded close to their friend and peered at the card.

"It looks like a regular invitation," said Flora.

"That's what would make it such a good joke," replied Nikki. "It doesn't look suspicious at all — so I show up at Tanya's house with last-year's swimsuit, and then Tanya and her friends all laugh at me, like who am I to think I've been invited to swim in Tanya's fancy pool?"

Olivia wrinkled her nose. "But why bother? Tanya never did anything *that* mean to us."

"She probably *is* having a party," said Flora, "and her mother made her invite all the girls in our class. If we went home and checked the mail, I'll bet we'd find invitations for Olivia and me, too."

"Really?" said Nikki.

"Definitely," Flora and Olivia both said at the same time.

"Okay. Can we go right now?"

Five minutes later, the girls, sharing a giant umbrella loaned to them by Gigi, were walking down Main Street, Olivia slurping her sandaled feet through every puddle she saw.

"Hey, Nikki," said Olivia, "what did you mean when you said you sure have been getting some interesting mail at your house? What else came?"

"Tobias got a letter from a college. A little college in Connecticut. Leavitt College, I think he said. It turns out that he secretly applied to a couple of colleges and was wait-listed at Leavitt. He just found out that there's a place for him there this fall *and* he's eligible for a scholarship."

"Wow," said Flora. "What's he going to do?"

"I don't know," replied Nikki. "I mean, it's funny. He never thought about going to college. When my dad was living with us, we just . . . didn't think about things like that. College was part of some other world. But now Dad is gone, and Mom is in charge. And she's changed so much — I mean in a good way — that she's like another person, really. So anyway, Tobias applied to these colleges, not thinking he would actually get in to them, at least not so soon, and now he has this big decision to make."

The girls had turned onto Aiken Avenue. They passed the Morrises' house, then Mr. Willet's, then the Malones', and Flora burst out from under the umbrella and ran up her walk. She reached into the mailbox, shuffled through the envelopes she pulled out, and crowed, "Ha! I got one! See?"

Nikki grinned. "Okay. I feel better. Go get yours, Olivia, and then I'll feel totally fine."

Olivia sprinted across the wet grass to her own mailbox. "Hmm," she said as she riffled through a stack of envelopes and catalogs. "I don't see one."

"Look again," said Flora. "You must have missed it. You have more mail than we do."

Olivia looked carefully at every envelope. "There's nothing for me," she said after a moment.

"Well, it'll probably come tomorrow," said Nikki. "You know how the mail is."

"I guess," said Olivia.

Olivia made a point of being at home when the mail was delivered the next day. Her letter carrier was still striding away from the Walters' door when Olivia snatched the mail from the box. No invitation.

There was no invitation the next day, either. Olivia plunked down on her front stoop and allowed Wednesday's mail to spill across her lap. She rested her elbows on her knees and her chin in her hands.

Left out again. Only this time it was worse than not being invited to Meagan's skating party in second grade or Jilly's sleepover in fourth grade, because then she hadn't had best friends who *had* been invited.

Olivia's thoughts strayed to September and the start of school — of seventh grade in the big central school for grades seven through twelve, serving students from elementary schools in all the surrounding small towns. A huge school. With the high schoolers right there. Right there with their makeup and iPods and dances and guys who needed to shave.

Olivia buried her face in her hands.


"What do you mean, you weren't invited?" exclaimed Ruby shrilly, her hands on her hips.

Olivia knew Ruby was partly acting (she did indeed look convincingly indignant), but partly truly upset on Olivia's behalf.

"I mean that those guys" (Olivia indicated Nikki and Flora, who were sprawled across Olivia's bed in the direct path of an energetically whirling fan) "got invitations days ago, and I didn't get one."

"Maybe yours got lost in the mail," said Ruby.

Olivia made a face. "I highly doubt that."

Ruby, who had been sitting at Olivia's desk, examining the intricate butterflies on a mobile, suddenly gasped and jumped to her feet.

"What's the matter?" asked Flora, looking alarmed.

"I just thought of something!" cried Ruby. "What if, um . . ." She paused. "Olivia, what if you weren't invited because of, you know . . . your skin color?"

Olivia gazed out the window. "There are probably a lot of reasons Tanya doesn't want me at her party, but that isn't one of them."

Ruby looked at Flora and Nikki on the bed. They were shaking their heads.

"Nope," said Nikki. "Olivia's right. Tanya is half African-American and half Japanese. Skin color doesn't have anything to do with it."

"I was excluded," said Olivia, making a face, "not because I'm black, but because I don't fit in with any of the other kids in our class. I never have. Only you guys understand me."

"I guess it doesn't matter *why* you were left out," said Ruby. "You were still left out. And that isn't fair."

"Gigi would say that life isn't fair," replied Olivia. "And I guess she should know. She *has* been excluded from things because of her skin color."

"Well, I say that if Olivia wasn't invited to Tanya's party, then Nikki and I shouldn't go," said Flora. "We'll RSVP that we can't come." She sat up and folded her arms across her chest.

"Yeah!" exclaimed Ruby. "Good idea. I wish I'd been invited, so I could blow Tanya off, too."

"No. That doesn't seem right," said Olivia in a small voice. "I want Nikki and Flora to go. You guys will have fun. You shouldn't miss out because of me."

"But we barely know Tanya," said Nikki.

"There's another thing to consider," Olivia went on. "Nikki, if you and Flora snub Tanya, it isn't going to look very good. I mean, socially. Everything's going to be different when we start seventh grade, and you don't want to have a reputation as the girls who snubbed Tanya, who, I don't have to remind you, is one of the more popular girls in our grade. There's no reason all three of us should start off on the wrong foot at our new school. Who knows what cliques and things will form there. It might be good if you're friends with Tanya and the other girls. You guys should go to the party."

Grudgingly, Flora and Nikki agreed with Olivia.

That night, Olivia sat alone in her bedroom. She pictured Nikki and Flora swimming in Tanya's pool, laughing with their new friends. She pictured them in the fall, being invited to other parties, to dances, to sleepovers. In all of Olivia's fearful imaginings about going to the central school, it had never entered her mind that Flora and Nikki might be pulled away from her. What would she do without them?

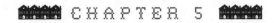 

# CHAPTER 5

# Ruby's Great Idea

Ruby Northrop stepped out of Needle and Thread and sat on the bench in front of the window. She made up a little song and sang it aloud to a tune she remembered from day camp, a tune about a dog named Bingo: *"There was a day in summertime when Ruby had no plans-oh. B-O-R-E-D, B-O-R-E-D, B-O-R-E-D, and Ruby had no plans!"* Ruby edged closer to the open door and sang more loudly: *"THERE WAS A DAY IN SUMMERTIME WHEN RUBY HAD NO PLANS-OH. B-O-R-E-D, B-O-R-E-D, B-O-R-E-D, AND RUBY HAD NO PLANS!"*

"Ruby," called Min from within the store. "Please come here for a moment."

Ruby sighed. She had wanted Min to hear her, but now she felt nervous about the tone of Min's voice.

"What," said Ruby flatly as she reentered the store.

"Any person," Min began, taking Ruby by the elbow and seating her on one of the couches, "with all the brains and personality you were lucky enough to have bestowed upon you, should not be bored. There is no good reason for it."

"But I don't have chorus or rehearsals or *any*thing until Turbo Tappers begins."

"What about the book club?" asked Min.

"I read *The Saturdays*."

"And *Mrs. Frisby*?"

"I have partially read *Mrs. Frisby*," Ruby replied cautiously.

"How about finishing it?"

"It's at home."

Min drew in a very deep breath and then said slowly, "Ruby. If you *want* to be bored, that can be accomplished easily. But so can not being bored. Go to the art store and buy a crafts kit. I'll lend you the money. Think about your 'green' project. Write a play. Go to the library. Call Lacey Morris and see what she's doing. You are smart, Ruby." Min tapped her head. "*Smart*. And creative. So please find something to do."

"I think," said Ruby, rising from the couch, "that I'll take a walk."

"Stay on Main Street," said Min.

Ruby didn't reply. She walked out of the store, and Min turned to Gigi and said, "Saints preserve us."

Ruby turned right when she left Needle and Thread.

Maybe, she thought, she would go into every store in town. That would be a good project. And it would probably take up the rest of the day. It was too bad she didn't have more money with her.

Ruby poked her head into Zack's, the hardware store. Hardware stores held little interest for her, but Olivia had told her that if she peeked through the knotholes in the old wooden floor, she could see down into the basement below. What might a person see in an ancient basement? Ruby walked up and down the aisles of Zack's until she found what she thought was the biggest knothole in the store. She lay on her stomach, closed her left eye, and pressed her right eye to the hole.

"Who goes there?" said a loud voice.

Ruby jumped. She widened her right eye and stared and stared into the darkness, wondering what kind of basement creature said, "Who goes there?"

"Hello?" called Ruby.

"Hello?" said the voice, and Ruby felt a tap on her shoulder. She pulled her head up and scrambled to her feet. Zack was standing behind her.

"Looking for treasure?" he asked.

Ruby blushed. "No, just . . . looking."

Ruby left Zack's in a hurry. She wandered through Heaven, glancing aimlessly at the jewelry. Already, the prospect of visiting *every* store on Main Street seemed less exciting.

Next to Heaven, though, was Sincerely Yours, Olivia's store. Ruby had barely entered when Robby Edwards called loudly, "Good afternoon, Ruby!"

"Hi, Robby," Ruby replied.

"Are you here to get a basket? I can help you. Do you need a birthday basket for someone? How about this birthday mug and some chocolates and look at these funny hats. We just got them in." Robby proudly led Ruby to a shelf near the cash register. "These are all new items," he told her.

Ruby looked around at the Walters' store. Olivia's parents sold candies and baked goods (made by Mrs. Walter) and everything a person could need to create a gift basket for any occasion. Robby had been working in the store for several weeks. It was his first job ever, and he took it seriously.

Ruby held out her empty hands. "I don't have any money," she said. She felt in her pocket. "Well, I have a little. But I'm just walking around."

"Can I offer you a piece of chocolate?" asked Olivia's father from behind the counter.

"Yes, thank you," replied Ruby, who never, ever turned down free candy. She selected a peanut butter patty.

Ruby emerged from the cool of the store into the sticky warmth of the afternoon. Immediately, she could feel the last bite of her candy grow melty and slidey in her fingers. She thrust it into her mouth. Then she stood in the shade, savoring the last of the chocolate, and looked across the street at Time and Again, the used bookstore. The display in the window read FUN IN THE SUN — SUPER SUMMERTIME READING! Ruby didn't care much about summertime reading, but she thought she would see whether Sonny Sutphin was working in the store.

She crossed Main Street and pushed open the door to Time and Again. And there was Sonny, sitting in his wheelchair behind the information desk. He was talking to Ruby's aunt Allie.

"Hi!" said Ruby, surprised to find her aunt in the store.

"Ruby!" exclaimed Allie, sounding equally surprised.

Aunt Allie, the younger sister of Ruby and Flora's mother, was a writer. A writer of books for grown-ups and famous in some circles, Min said. Which Ruby took to mean it was okay that she had never heard of any of her aunt's books. Allie had long lived in New York City, and Ruby had thought she must be terribly glamorous. Then Allie had come home to Camden Falls for Christmas the previous year, and Ruby had been dismayed to meet an uncomfortable, serious, and generally unappealing adult, one whose interest in food ran to tasteless, cardboardlike organic products, and whose lips would never admit a Twinkie or a cheese puff. Ruby was further dismayed when Allie announced that she

had decided to remain in Camden Falls permanently —
and she ended up living with Ruby, Flora, and Min for
months while she house hunted. Now, at long last, Allie
had a home of her own, and Ruby's gratefulness knew
no bounds.

But what was Aunt Allie doing out shopping in the
middle of the day when she should be working? She was
a very disciplined person (no surprise there), and, when
she had lived at the Row House, had been capable of
becoming quite crabby if Ruby or Flora interrupted
her writing schedule.

This was probably why Aunt Allie now looked so
startled to see Ruby enter Time and Again. Caught!
Ruby had caught her aunt out shopping when, according to Allie's own schedule, she should be at home
clacking away on her laptop.

"Hi," said Ruby a second time. And then, not want-
ing to get caught up in a dreary conversation with her
aunt, had added, "Well, I have to go now. See you
later."

Ruby ran out of the store. To be safe, she crossed
Main Street again, ran by Needle and Thread, and then
crossed Dodds Lane. There. That should put enough
distance between her and her aunt. Ruby realized that
she was now standing in front of the site of the fire. She
was looking at the building (the windows of Plaza
Drugs, Hulit's, and the diner were temporarily boarded
up, so she couldn't see much) when around the corner

came the family who had bought the Marquis. What were their names? Ruby had been introduced to them on the day Min and Gigi had invited them to Needle and Thread for coffee. Nelson, that was their last name. And the kids were Hilary and Spencer.

"Hi," said Ruby. "Remember me?"

Hilary regarded her seriously. "Is your name Ruby?" she asked.

Ruby nodded.

"Hi, Ruby," said Mr. Nelson. "Nice to see you again." He turned to Hilary and Spencer. "Kids, you wait outside while your mother and I check on the repairs."

"Darn," said Spencer, sitting right down on the sidewalk. "I wanted to go inside. You know what Mom and Dad get to wear in there? Hard hats. I want a hard hat."

Hilary sighed, said nothing, and squatted next to her brother.

"Um," said Ruby, "so . . ." She thought for a moment. "So where are you living now?" She recalled that the Nelsons had been living above the ruined diner. She raised her eyes to more boarded-up windows.

"In a house on Pond Road," said Hilary.

"It has a swing in the backyard!" said Spencer.

"But we're just renting the house," added Hilary. "It isn't ours."

"Oh. How old are you?" asked Ruby.

"Ten."

"Will you be in fifth grade this fall?"

"Yup."

"At Camden Falls Elementary?"

Hilary nodded.

"Then maybe you'll be in my class!" said Ruby. "You'll be in my grade."

"If we're still here," said Hilary.

"What?" asked Ruby.

Hilary glanced at her brother. "Hey, Spencer," she said. "Why don't you go sit on that bench? Here's your Game Boy. Mom said you could play it for fifteen minutes."

Spencer snatched the Game Boy from his sister and ran for the bench.

When he was staring intently at the screen, Hilary said quietly to Ruby, "We don't really have enough money to stay here. We spent all our money buying the diner and fixing it up."

Ruby frowned. "I thought Min said — Min is my grandmother — I thought she said your insurance company would pay to fix up the diner."

"They'll pay for some things but not everything," said Hilary. "And they're not paying for us to rent a house." She glanced at Ruby, then lowered her voice to a whisper. "I'm not supposed to talk about this. I'm not even really supposed to know what's going on. But I'm a worrier. That's what my parents say. So I know *exactly* what's going on. Mom and Dad spent all of our savings on the diner. They wanted us to live in a small town. They thought it would be better for Spencer and me to grow up here. Which I guess it is. But . . ." (Hilary spread her hands) "now we have nothing. No money. I don't even know how Mom and Dad were able to rent the house. They must have borrowed money from someone. If we can't make things work here, I don't know what we'll do. Maybe move back to Boston and live with my grandparents."

"Wow," said Ruby. "Really?" She stood up and peered through the door to the murky interior of the Marquis Diner. She tried to recall what it had looked like before the fire. She had a dim memory of a long polished counter, booths with red vinyl seats, and on the walls, posters advertising Broadway shows. There had been photos of actors, too, and a board on which were listed the sandwiches the Marquis served. The sandwiches were named for famous people. Ruby wished for a sandwich named the Ruby Reuben. And after she became a famous Broadway actor herself, her own photo could go on the wall. Maybe right next to the cash register, where everyone would be sure to see it. But none of those things would happen if the Nelsons weren't able to go ahead with their plans. Their *dreams*, Ruby reminded herself, and immediately felt selfish for so much as thinking about her star photo and the Ruby Reuben.

Ruby turned back to Hilary. She saw a frail girl,

small for her age, with very sad eyes. An image of Timothy Frisby, the sick mouse child in *Mrs. Frisby and the Rats of NIMH*, came to Ruby's mind. How bravely and earnestly Timothy's mother, Mrs. Frisby, had fought to save his life. She had done things she didn't know she was capable of, and in the end, an entire community had rallied to help the Frisbys.

Ruby turned her gaze down Main Street. She thought about the fact that Min knew the owner of just about every store and business in town. Then Ruby realized that she herself knew lots of the people who worked in the stores. And those people were a community, the Main Street community.

Ruby could feel her heart begin to pound. "Hilary," she said, "I'd better go. I have to check in with my grandmother." (Not true.) "Come stop by our store anytime, okay? I'm there a lot. Unfortunately."

Hilary grinned, and Ruby realized it was the first time she had seen her smile. "Okay," said Hilary.

Ruby ran back across Dodds Lane. By the time she reached Dutch Haus on the opposite corner, an idea was taking shape in her brain. She pushed her way into the store. "Jeanne!" she said to the woman behind the counter. "You know the Nelsons? Whose diner burned down? I think we should have a big event to help raise money for them! The whole town could help out." Ruby tried to relate in a calm and orderly fashion what she had learned from Hilary.

"Why, that's a wonderful idea, Ruby," said Jeanne. "Let me put on my thinking cap. I know we can come up with something."

"I'm going to go talk to everyone else!" said Ruby breathlessly.

And that is what she did. Ruby spent the rest of the afternoon stopping in at the stores on Main Street. She talked to Frank in Frank's Beans. She talked to Sonny in Time and Again. She talked to the Walters in Sincerely Yours. She even talked to the odious Mrs. Grindle in Stuff 'n' Nonsense. Then she talked to people in the T-shirt Emporium and the Cheshire Cat and the grocery store, and to the Fongs at their studio.

At last, exhausted but quite pleased with herself, Ruby returned to Needle and Thread and told Min and Gigi her idea for helping the Nelsons get back on their feet.

Min looked a bit startled. "You've already told the whole town about this?" she exclaimed.

"Oh. Should I have told you first?" said Ruby.

Min smiled and shook her head. "Never mind. I think your idea is terrific. If we all put our heads together, I know we'll think of the perfect project."

"Exactly."

"Are you bored now?" asked Min.

"Bored?" said Ruby. "What's that?"

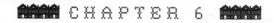 

# CHAPTER 6

# Project Green

Nikki Sherman was sitting and thinking. She liked sitting and thinking, especially on a clear, warm Saturday, when she could sit and think in peace on her front stoop. Nikki breathed in the summertime smells: honeysuckle and clover and sun-drenched grass. She leaned over and pinched a bit of lavender from the plant by the stoop, then breathed in its scent. "Heavenly," she said aloud, and, eyes closed, was transported to her mother's bedroom. On summer mornings, Nikki liked to lie on Mrs. Sherman's bed and watch her get ready for work. The last thing Mrs. Sherman would do, before taking one final glance in the mirror, was pour a drop of lavender oil from the purple glass bottle on her dresser and dab it behind each ear. Lavender was the scent of Nikki's mother.

On the stoop next to Nikki were her copies of *The Saturdays* and *Mrs. Frisby*. Nikki was waiting for Mr. Walter to bring Olivia, Ruby, and Flora by. The girls planned to spend the afternoon at Nikki's — the first of their special Saturdays. Nikki had been looking forward to this day, but she had a feeling that the Melendys' adventures would surpass any adventures the members of the secret book club would share this summer. Just for starters, the Melendys lived in Manhattan (a fact that was bound to impress Ruby), and they had such things as museums and opera houses at hand. What was at hand in tiny Camden Falls? wondered Nikki. Then she scolded herself. Who knew what summer adventures lay ahead? Her own Saturdays might well be as exciting as the Melendys'.

Nikki's ears caught the sound of a car on the road, and moments later she saw a small cloud of dust as Mr. Walter's Toyota rumbled along the dirt road to the Shermans' house.

"Bye, girls! Have fun," said Olivia's father as Flora, Ruby, and Olivia scrambled out of the car and ran to Nikki.

"Bye!" chorused the girls. And Olivia added, "Remember, Min is going to pick us up later."

Mr. Walter honked his horn. Then he turned the car around and headed back to Main Street.

The four girls, holding their books, now stood awkwardly in front of the Shermans' house.

"So," said Olivia, looking uncertainly at her friends. "How do you think we start our first meeting?"

"I guess we talk about the books," said Flora.

Nikki consulted the letter that had accompanied the books. "And then we think about our green project."

"Are we supposed to hold an actual meeting?" asked Olivia. "Is someone supposed to call it to order?"

"What do people in book clubs *do*?" asked Ruby.

"They have *fun*," said a voice from behind the screen door. The door opened and Tobias stepped outside. "You girls are so *serious*," he went on. "Just grab some sodas from the fridge, go up to Nikki's room, and lie around on the beds. Isn't that what girls do when they get together? Have some bonding time or something?" (Flora giggled.) "Anyway, you guys are on your own. I'm going to take Mae over to the Shaws' for a while."

"We're going to look for fish in their pond!" exclaimed Mae giddily as she charged through the door and joined her brother on the stoop.

Five minutes later, Tobias and Mae were gone, and Nikki, Flora, Ruby, and Olivia were doing what Tobias suggested: They were sprawled around the room Nikki and Mae shared, drinking sodas. Flora, book club letter in hand, led off the conversation with, "Okay, the first thing to talk about is Mrs. Frisby and bravery," but she was interrupted by Ruby, who said, "I hope we're not going to follow the letter *exactly*, like a worksheet in school. Let's just talk about the books. And I say, let's start with *The Saturdays*, even though it's our bonus book, and all the questions and everything are about *Mrs. Frisby*."

"Ruby," said Flora, a note of suspicion in her voice, "you did read *Mrs. Frisby*, didn't you?"

"I loved the first twelve chapters!" said Ruby rapturously.

"What about the rest of the chapters?" asked Olivia.

Ruby paused. "I'm sure I'll like them just as much."

"Ruby! Our very first meeting and you didn't even finish the book!" exclaimed Flora.

"How could you stop in the middle?" cried Olivia. "I think *Mrs. Frisby and the Rats of NIMH* might possibly be the most exciting book I ever read!"

"Well, to begin with, there were *two* books. And *Mrs. Frisby* is very long," said Ruby. "The printing is tiny," she added. "Teeny-tiny. The printing in *The Saturdays* is much better and easier to read."

There was a brief silence, after which Olivia said, "The sad thing is that Ruby doesn't even know what a great story she missed. I feel very bad for her."

"Hey!" Ruby cried. "That is not your business, Olivia. It's mine."

"No, you're wrong. It's *our* business. Aren't all the members of a book club supposed to read the books so that they have a shared experience? If we all read *Mrs. Frisby*, for instance, then we've all — *all*," she repeated, looking at Ruby, "shared that experience. We have it in common."

"Bonding," said Flora. "Tobias was kidding, but I think he has a point."

"Can't we bond over *The Saturdays*?" asked Ruby.

"Look, you guys," said Nikki. "Let's just start talking about the books, okay? If Ruby can join in, great. If she can't, well, maybe she'll want to finish future books." (It was Nikki's turn to eye Ruby.) "And I don't think," she added hastily, glancing at Flora and Olivia, "that we have to talk about every single thing listed in the letter. Let's just use the letter as a guide. I think the main purpose of this particular club is to have some fun adventures this summer."

"Like the Melendys," said Ruby pointedly. "And don't you guys think it's good that I at least finished one book?"

"Yes," said Flora.

"You want to know what my favorite part of *The Saturdays* was?" asked Ruby. "It was when Oliver went to the circus. All by himself, and he was only six years old. I know it was naughty, but that's why I liked it. Also, I liked it when he came home with the policeman and puked on the doormat."

Olivia laughed. "I liked the part when Rush found the dog. I wish I had a dog."

"I liked that the Melendys were so independent," said Nikki.

"Do you think all New York kids are as independent as they are?" asked Ruby dreamily.

"Not nowadays," said Flora. "Did you guys notice when this book was published? Way back in 1941. I'll bet things were really different then. I'll bet New York kids couldn't do any of those things today. Not by themselves, like the Melendys did. A grown-up would have to go with them on their Saturday adventures now."

"I think *that's* sad," said Ruby. "I'll bet we're more independent here in Camden Falls than kids our age in New York City."

"That's funny," said Nikki, "because while I was waiting for you guys to come over, I was feeling a little jealous of the Melendys and their adventures, but now I don't feel so bad."

"Do you think the Melendys showed bravery on their adventures or were they just having fun?" asked Olivia. "I was looking at the first thing to talk about in the letter — about bravery in *Mrs. Frisby* — and I was about to say that Mrs. Frisby showed a lot of bravery while the Melendys just had fun, but then I realized that might not be true."

"I think the Melendys mostly had fun," said Flora, "but some of the things they did were brave, too. I mean, it's kind of silly, but when Mona got her hair cut, that was brave."

"Not nearly as brave as what Mrs. Frisby did to save Timothy!" exclaimed Ruby. She turned to Olivia. "See? I can still contribute to our discussion." Olivia smiled a tiny smile. "Mrs. Frisby had to brave Dragon the cat," Ruby continued, "and Jeremy the crow, and the owl — I don't think we ever find out the owl's name, do we? Anyway, Mrs. Frisby was *really* brave."

"But when Mona cut her hair, it changed her identity," said Flora. "That's brave, too, just in a different kind of way."

"Overall, though," said Olivia, "I think there was more bravery in *Mrs. Frisby*. The rats were brave when they were trapped in the cages at NIMH."

"Mrs. Frisby's husband had been brave," said Nikki. "That's why the rats were so nice to Mrs. Frisby when Timothy was sick."

"Nicodemus the rat was brave," said Flora. "He came up with the plan for the rats' escape."

"There's something I've been wondering," said Nikki. "This isn't in the letter, but I can't stop thinking about it: Do you believe that the seven rats who died in the hardware store were Jenner and his group, who split off from the others? You know, the renegade rats? Because if they weren't, then they could still be out there, planning to —"

"Stop!" cried Ruby. "Don't say another word! You mean Jenner wants to come back and get revenge on Nicodemus or something?"

"Do you really want us to answer your question or do you want to finish the book?" asked Olivia.

"Now I want to finish the book. So don't talk about anything that will give away the rest of the story."

At this, Flora looked highly put out, but Nikki said, "Wait. Here's something we can discuss that won't give the end away." She read from the paper. "'Tell your friends about something you did that was brave.'"

Ruby jumped up. "I am brave every time I stand on a stage in front of an audience."

Flora frowned. "Really? I thought you liked being onstage."

"I do," said Ruby, "but it's still brave." She sat down.

There was a little silence and then Olivia said, "I felt like I had to be brave when my parents were out of work and didn't know what they wanted to do." She paused. "Actually, I felt like I *should* have been brave, but I wasn't really, so I guess that doesn't count. I don't feel like a brave person."

"Me, neither," said Flora. "But I think I was brave the night of the car accident. Ruby and I were at the hospital and we knew something bad had happened to Mom and Dad, and then this police officer started asking me all these questions about who to contact in an emergency. So I told myself I had to be brave for Ruby and stay strong and take care of things." Flora looked at Nikki. "What about you?"

"Something about my father," muttered Nikki, "but I don't want to talk about it."

The girls didn't press their friend. They talked instead about the characters in *Mrs. Frisby* and which ones they were most like. They wanted to talk about what might have happened after the end of the story but were hampered by Ruby's insistence that they not ruin the last sixteen chapters for her. So finally Olivia said, "Well, what about our project — to help make Camden Falls a greener place?"

"What does a green project have to do with *Mrs. Frisby*?" asked Ruby.

"You'd know if you'd finished the book," said Flora.

"You'll find out," added Nikki in a kinder tone of voice, "when you get to the part about the rat race."

"All right," said Ruby, sounding contrite. "I guess the point is that we have to think of something to do to make our town greener. But what *can* we do? We're just kids."

"The rats were 'just rats' and they thought of something," said Olivia.

"Hey, I know!" exclaimed Nikki. "How about if we plant a vegetable garden?" She turned to Ruby. "That will make more sense to you after you finish the book."

"Oh, that's a good idea," said Flora. "And we could

keep some of the vegetables for ourselves, but we could donate the rest of them to the food bank — to help feed people who don't have enough to eat."

"This is great," said Olivia. "I love it. But is it too late to start a vegetable garden? It's almost July. And what's that old saying? Corn is supposed to be knee-high by the Fourth of July? Our corn would have to grow awfully quickly to catch up."

"Plus, we don't know anything about vegetable gardening," pointed out Ruby.

"But I know who does," said Olivia. "Mr. Pennington."

"Let's call him!" said Nikki.

So Olivia phoned him but got no answer.

"Well, I think we can do it anyway," said Flora. "This is going to be fun. What should we plant?"

Flora, Olivia, Nikki, and Ruby made lists and charts. They looked up the answers to several questions on the Shermans' computer. They called the food bank. They made more lists. By the time Min's car pulled up, Ruby was bouncy with energy and plans. So when, to the girls' surprise, Mr. Pennington climbed out of the passenger seat, Ruby ran to him, nearly knocking him off his feet.

"Mr. Pennington! I can't believe you're here! We tried to call you! We're going to start a vegetable garden! For the food bank!"

Ruby's words tumbled out in such a rush that Flora had to step in and give Mr. Pennington and Min a more coherent explanation.

"Well, I think I can help you out," said Mr. Pennington. "It is a bit late to be starting a garden, but you can do it."

He answered the girls' questions patiently, and by the time Min said that they really had better be on their way, the girls had decided exactly what they needed for their garden, and Olivia had suggested that the garden be planted in her backyard, conveniently next door to Mr. Pennington in case his help was needed. "Which," said Olivia, "I'm sure it will be."

At last Min's car, now carrying five people, drove down Nikki's lane. As Nikki watched it disappear in the distance, a slow smile spread across her face. This Saturday, she said to herself, had been as much fun as any of the Melendys'.

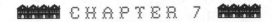 

# CHAPTER 7

# *Party Girls*

Ruby stood in the doorway to Flora's room and peered inside curiously. "Flora?" she said. "What are you doing?"

Flora's bed was heaped with clothes. So was her floor. And her armchair. Clothes had been flung everywhere. The room looked like a beach after a storm. The only spot empty of clothes was the wardrobe, in which, as far as Ruby knew, all of these same clothes had been neatly folded or hanging just the night before.

"I'm trying to find something to wear," answered Flora.

"For *gar*dening?" Ruby looked down at her own body, which was clad in a T-shirt and a pair of jeans. The shirt sported a ring of tiny holes around the neck binding, and the jeans smelled faintly of the outdoors; when Ruby studied them more closely, she saw grass stains on the knees. These were not Ruby's best clothes (she had, in fact, pulled the shirt out of Min's ragbag), but they were perfect for gardening.

"No!" cried Flora. "Not for gardening. For the party tonight. Tanya's party."

"Oh." Ruby lifted a white blouse from the edge of Flora's bed, moved it to a pile of skirts, and sat in the empty space. "So you and Nikki are definitely going?"

Flora didn't answer right away. She appeared to be studying a pink-and-green-flowered sundress. At last she replied, "Yes. We talked about it again with Olivia. You know, Nikki and I don't really want to go, but we thought it would send some kind of message if we decided to stay home on account of Olivia."

"Couldn't you have just said you can't go because you're already busy?"

"Yes. But then Tanya wouldn't have known the real reason we stayed home."

"But I thought you didn't want her to know!" exclaimed Ruby. "And anyway, aren't you sending her another kind of message by accepting her invitation even though she didn't ask Olivia to the party?"

Flora sighed. "It's all very complicated." She tossed the sundress onto her bed. "I'll decide about my outfit later. Come on. Let's go to Olivia's. After all, it's another Saturday."

"And we have a vegetable garden to plant," added Ruby.

Ruby thought about the past week. She and Flora and Olivia and Nikki had been busy. And they had worked hard. First they had gotten permission from Olivia's parents to plant their garden in the Walters' backyard. Then, with plenty of help from Mr. Pennington, they had staked out a plot, pulled up the grass, turned the earth over, and begun to prepare the soil.

"Since it's so late in the season," said Mr. Pennington, "you won't have time to start your plants from seeds. You'll need to buy seedlings at the garden center. Those are already sprouted plants."

Ruby, grubby from her work in the garden, had glanced at her equally grubby sister and their friends. "We also have to buy ... what did you say, Mr. Pennington? What's that stuff we need to put in the dirt?"

"You'll probably want some peat moss and organic fertilizer to turn into the soil before you begin planting."

Ruby had thought sadly of her piggy bank. "I only have two dollars and forty cents in the hog," she said. "How much money do the rest of you guys have?"

"Not much," said Olivia.

"Hardly anything," said Nikki.

"Next to nothing," said Flora.

"Well, how are we going to buy all this stuff?" wondered Ruby.

This conversation had taken place on Monday afternoon in Olivia's backyard. The very next day, an envelope had mysteriously appeared on the counter at Needle and Thread. On the front was written:

FLORA
RUBY
OLIVIA
NIKKI

Gigi had picked it up, said, "What's this?" and given it to Flora.

Flora frowned at the handwriting, which she didn't recognize. Then she opened the envelope and inside found several twenty-dollar bills and a brief note, in the same handwriting, stating that the money was for supplies for the girls' green project. Gigi and Min protested that they knew nothing about the money and had no idea when or how the envelope had arrived. Flora was inclined to believe them.

The next day, Mr. Pennington had driven the girls to the garden center and helped them select the peat moss and fertilizer, as well as a few tools.

"What about the seedlings?" Ruby had asked.

"We'll come back on Friday and buy them then," Mr. Pennington replied. "We don't want them sitting around for too long before they go in the ground."

On Friday, they had returned to the garden center

and bought seedlings for green peppers, two kinds of tomatoes, broccoli, eggplant, two kinds of squash, radishes, cucumbers, spinach, and lettuce.

"And the corn?" asked Olivia. "What about the corn? We could buy knee-high seedlings to stay on schedule."

Mr. Pennington smiled. "No corn," he said. "Corn needs lots and lots of room. You don't have enough space to grow corn properly in your garden. But you'll have plenty of other good things."

And now it was the morning of the girls' next Saturday adventure. Ruby was looking forward to planting the garden. Shortly after lunch, she and Flora ran next door to Olivia's house. Nikki arrived at the same time, and the girls met Mr. Pennington in the backyard. Moments later, Ruby found herself standing at the edge of their garden, a tray of spinach seedlings in her hands.

"Use the trowel to dig nice little holes," Mr. Pennington said. "Just about the size of each section of the tray. Then carefully lift the plant out and put it in the hole, dirt and all. We'll water the garden as soon as all the plants are in."

Planting the seedlings took less time than Ruby had thought it might take. Even so, the girls and Mr. Pennington were still hooking up the sprinkler and tidying the Walters' yard when Flora said, "Well, um,

I'm sorry to say this, but I guess Nikki and I have to go now. Can you guys finish up?"

"Sure!" said Olivia brightly. "Of course we can! Don't mind us."

Ruby watched Flora and Nikki as they began to edge toward Min's house.

Mr. Pennington, who was kneeling in the garden, glanced up, curious. "What's going on?" he asked.

Ruby whispered in his ear, "It's a whole big thing. I'll tell you later."

Mr. Pennington pinched back a smile and resumed adjusting the sprinkler.

"Well . . . bye," called Flora from Min's yard.

"See you!" said Olivia cheerfully. But she didn't look at Flora and Nikki. Instead, she continued collecting the empty seedling containers.

"I'll call you tomorrow," said Nikki.

"Fine," Olivia replied. Ruby thought she heard her add a muttered "Whatever."

"Olivia, you know, Nikki and I could always —" Flora started to say, but Olivia flung the containers onto the grass, stomped on them furiously, and cried, "Go! Just go, okay?"

Flora and Nikki let themselves into Min's house and closed the back door quietly behind them.

Mr. Pennington, looking from one to another of the girls, rose stiffly to his feet. He stood for a moment, rubbing his knees. "Well," he said, "maybe I should be on my way, too. Olivia? Everything all right?"

"Yes," said Olivia curtly. Then she added, "Really. It's okay, Mr. Pennington."

"Olivia and I have the whole rest of the afternoon planned," announced Ruby.

"We do?" said Olivia.

"Yes," said Ruby, even though the thought had just occurred to her. "We're having our *own* Saturday."

"Ah, *The Saturdays*," said Mr. Pennington fondly. Mr. Pennington had once taught in the very same elementary school Ruby now attended, a fact that fascinated her.

"Hey, Mr. Pennington," said Ruby as her previously unformed plans now began to take shape in her mind, "would you like to have a book discussion with Olivia and me? I have just finished reading a, um, an in*trigu*ing book called *Mrs. Frisby and the Rats of NIMH*."

"You finished it?" asked Olivia in surprise.

Ruby nodded proudly. "It had very small print," she informed Mr. Pennington. "But it was worth it."

"I have an idea," said Mr. Pennington. "Why don't you two come over and we'll have the discussion in my yard? Jacques would like to see you."

"So that's what we did," Ruby told Flora that evening. "I mean, we cleaned up — Olivia and I — and then we went to Mr. Pennington's and sat in his yard and talked about the book. It was great."

"You enjoyed a book talk," said Flora, managing to sound both dubious and incredulous at the same time.

"It's not an impossibleness."

"Impossibility," Flora corrected her automatically.

"Okay." Ruby, perched on Flora's bed in the once-again impeccably tidy room, said, "Well?"

"Well what?"

"You know what! The party! Tell me everything about the party!"

Flora gazed soberly out her dark window. "It was fun," she said at last.

"That's it? It was fun?"

"Ruby, sometimes it's kind of hard to put my thoughts and feelings into words," said Flora in her most annoying older-sister way.

"Just start by telling me what you did."

"Okay. Well, when we first arrived, everyone —"

"How many people were already there?" interrupted Ruby.

"About five or six. Anyway, everyone was out back by Tanya's pool. First we just swam for a while and talked and stuff. Then Tanya's parents put hamburgers and hot dogs and chicken on the barbecue. We ate dinner at two picnic tables."

"Did you and Nikki stick together the whole time?" asked Ruby.

"Not the whole time. We both knew everyone there."

"Were *all* the other kids from your class there except for Olivia?"

"Not all," replied Flora. "But most of them. I don't know if the others were away or what. And then there were about five girls from Mrs. Annich's class." (Mrs. Annich was the other sixth-grade teacher at Camden Falls Elementary.)

"So you had fun?" prompted Ruby.

"Yes," said Flora. "I really did."

Flora remembered the jumpy feeling in her stomach when Min had dropped her and Nikki at Tanya's house. What if no one except Nikki spoke to her at the party? What if the invitations had been a bad joke after all? Flora had imagined dozens of horrifying situations — being snubbed, ignored, teased — but of course nothing even resembling these scenarios had taken place. She had merely swum and eaten chicken and chatted with the other girls. They talked about their summer plans and movies they'd seen. At one point, Tanya had whispered in Flora's ear, "Will Price has a crush on Sophie and she has one on him!"

Flora, smiling, had looked around at all her classmates — laughing, swimming, wiping barbecue sauce off their fingers — and thought with some surprise,

So now I'm part of this, too. She was part of her new family with Min and part of the Row Houses and part of Main Street and part of her small circle of friends. And now she was part of this bigger circle of girls.

This bigger circle, she had mused, did not include Olivia. Was that all right? (This was one of those thoughts she did not yet care to put into words for Ruby.) She supposed so. After all, even best friends couldn't stick together *all* the time. And in September, when Flora moved to the central school, she would be part of a much wider world. Why, she and Olivia might not even have any classes together. Still, she thought uncomfortably, Olivia had been her friend since the day she and Ruby had moved to Camden Falls and had helped to ease her into her new life.

"Flora?" said Ruby.

"Just thinking."

Ruby knew better than to ask what her sister was thinking about.

Across Camden Falls, in a house far out in the countryside, Nikki Sherman lay in her bed, Mae in deep sleep on the other side of the room. Nikki replayed the events of Tanya's party, marveling at the very fact that she'd been invited to it. She had had a wonderful time. As she drifted off to sleep, she tried not to recall the look on Olivia's face when Nikki and Flora had left her behind in the vegetable garden that afternoon.

# CHAPTER 8

# Mr. Willet's Great Idea

"I'll get it! I'll get it!" cried Ruby the moment the telephone began to ring. She leaped to her feet and pounced on the phone, causing Daisy Dear to let out a bark of alarm, the hackles rising on her back.

"Ruby, calm down," said Flora. "Look what you made Daisy do."

"The *phone* made her do that," replied Ruby.

"It did not. She doesn't bark every time the phone rings."

Ruby turned her back on Flora. "Hello?" she said into the receiver.

Flora rolled her eyes and tried to remember if, when she was ten, a ringing telephone had inspired such commotion.

"Really?" Ruby was saying. "Oh, goody! We'll be right there. Thanks, Min. Bye!" Ruby clicked off the phone and turned to her sister. "They're here! I mean, they're at the store. Our next book club packages! I told Min we'd go get them."

Min Read was testing the waters with her grand-daughters. "Giving them their independence," Flora had heard her tell Mr. Pennington one evening. To that end, she now allowed the girls to be on their own every now and then, and Ruby was especially grateful. Flora, who actually enjoyed spending time at Needle and Thread, wasn't grateful so much as she was pleased to be deemed responsible enough to take charge of Ruby (an arrangement of which Ruby was unaware).

"Come on!" exclaimed Ruby. "Let's go!"

"Aren't you forgetting something?" asked Flora.

Ruby glanced around the living room. King Comma was asleep on a chair. Daisy Dear was now sitting plac-idly on another chair. Both had eaten breakfast, and Ruby had recently walked Daisy.

"No," said Ruby.

Flora regarded her silently.

"What?" cried Ruby.

"Don't you think we should call Olivia and Nikki and tell them about the packages, too?"

"Oh. Yeah."

Half an hour later, the four girls met at Needle and Thread, Nikki flushed from her long bicycle ride.

"This is so exciting!" said Nikki as the girls filed into the store.

"Yes. It's very exciting," said Olivia distantly.

Flora studied Olivia for a moment but said nothing. Tanya's party had taken place two days earlier, and Flora had seen little of Olivia since the planting of the vegetable garden.

Ruby took the packages from the counter and carried them to Nikki, Olivia, and Flora, who were sitting on the couches at the front of the store. Olivia, Ruby noted, was sitting by herself; Nikki and Flora were seated together on the other couch. Ruby considered the situation, then decided that unless all three girls were to sit on the same couch, *someone* had to sit alone. Still . . . why was it Olivia? Ruby flopped herself down next to Olivia, sorted through the envelopes, and handed Olivia's to her first.

When each girl was holding her package, Flora said, "Okay, one, two, three . . . go!"

In a flash, the packages were ripped open. Flora looked at the paperback book she had withdrawn. "*Roll of Thunder, Hear My Cry*," she said softly.

"By Mildred D. Taylor. I like the cover," said Nikki, studying it.

What Flora noticed first when she looked at the cover were the colors — oranges and browns, the colors of sunshine and earth.

"I almost didn't see the face," said Ruby suddenly, noticing the somber face of a young girl. "It blends right into the background."

"Not the background," said Flora. "The world, I think. The girl is immersed in her world. That's Cassie, by the way. And Cassie and the earth and the air — they're all connected, all part of one another. You'll understand when you read the book."

"You've already read it?" asked Olivia, sounding wounded.

Flora shrugged. "Last year. It's one of the best books ever. I'll be happy to read it again. And you guys are going to love it."

"I like that we can talk about the cover even though we haven't read the book yet," mused Ruby.

Flora shot Olivia an amused glance, but Olivia didn't return it.

Nikki looked from Olivia to Flora, then said, "Let's read the letters."

"I wonder what our next Saturday adventure will be," said Ruby.

"You read, Olivia," said Flora.

Without looking at the other girls, Olivia opened her copy of the letter. "Wow," she said after a moment. Then, "*Wow.*"

*Roll of Thunder* was the story of Cassie Logan, an African-American girl growing up in a loving family in Mississippi during the Depression, and of her family's fight to save their farm while at the same time battling bigotry and oppression during the tumultuous ninth year of Cassie's life. The list of things to talk about covered such topics as family relationships, Jim Crow laws, and the Underground Railroad.

"Why the Underground Railroad?" said Flora, looking confused.

And Ruby cried, "Jim Crow laws! That's a funny name. What are Jim Crow laws?"

"The Jim Crow laws are not funny, Ruby," said Olivia.

"In my mind they are." Ruby was picturing a human-size crow, dressed in judge's robes, presiding over a courtroom, wings flapping.

"The Jim Crow laws," said Olivia, "have to do with segregation and with discrimination against black people. When the laws were put in place, they were supposed to create separate but equal status for whites and blacks. The result was that black people not only had separate water fountains, separate seats in restaurants and theatres, separate schools, and so on, but that these things were *not* the same as those for white people. They were inferior. And the laws made black people feel like second-class citizens. How would you like to be really thirsty on a hot day and find a water fountain in a park, but then see the sign on the fountain that says WHITES ONLY?"

Flora thought Ruby looked a bit frightened. "Well," said Ruby after a moment. "Well . . . I'm sorry I made a joke about it, Olivia. Is this really what the book is about?"

"Sort of," said Flora, "but there's so much more to Cassie's story. Wait until you start reading about her family, especially Little Man, her younger brother. And it's a really exciting story. You won't believe what happens. What I can't figure out is why we're supposed to talk about the Underground Railroad. That isn't part of the book."

"Let's see what our Saturday adventure is," said Nikki. "Read that part of the letter, Olivia."

Olivia scanned the letter, then said, "Okay. Here it is. 'Two Saturdays from now, after you have read this compelling story and discussed it, sit down together and write one additional chapter to *Roll of Thunder, Hear My Cry*. Write about what you think happens to the characters in the years after the book ends. Be sure to include your thoughts about T.J.'" Olivia paused. "T.J.?"

"He's a really interesting character," said Flora. "You kind of want to not like him, but you can't. I mean, you can't hate him. Not really. Not that it's okay to hate anyone," she added hastily. "Well, I don't want to give the end away, but wait until you see what happens to T.J. I know why we're supposed to include him in our chapter."

"I've never written a chapter to a book before," said Nikki. "How are we going to do that?"

"We'll all be working together," Flora pointed out.

"It still sounds hard."

"I think it sounds like fun," said Olivia, who didn't look as though she was having any fun at all at the moment.

"We'll have to write a lot of pages," said Nikki.

"Believe me, there will be plenty to write about," said Flora.

"Is that it?" asked Ruby. "We just write a chapter? I have to say, this sounds kind of like homework. The Melendys never chose homework for their adventures."

"Nope, there's more." Olivia picked up the letter again. "Okay, let's see. We'll have to finish our chapter early in the afternoon, because at three o'clock we're supposed to . . . huh."

"What? What?" cried Ruby, scanning her copy of the letter.

"The letter says," Olivia continued, "'At three o'clock, ring the doorbell at number three fifty-seven Harmony Lane. The rest of your adventure will unfold from there. Don't worry — I've already spoken to your parents or grandparents about this and have their permission for you to go to the house.' Then the letter ends with, 'Enjoy your next Saturday adventure!'"

"Huh," said Nikki. "So Min and all our parents know who the secret book club person is."

"Where's Harmony Lane?" asked Flora.

Nikki shrugged, but Olivia said, "We can walk to it from the Row Houses."

"I wonder what a house on Harmony Lane has to do with *Roll of Thunder*," said Ruby.

Ruby, Nikki, and Flora turned to Olivia, but Olivia said, "Don't look at me. I only know about the Jim Crow laws."

"Hey, there's Mr. Willet!" exclaimed Ruby as the door to Needle and Thread opened. "Hi, Mr. Willet!"

Mr. Willet smiled at the girls, and Ruby and Olivia squinched over on the couch to make room for him.

"Are you here to buy something?" asked Ruby.

"No. I had an idea and I wanted to talk to your grandmother about it. Your grandmother, too, Olivia."

Mr. Willet's idea, it turned out, was to hold a series of sewing workshops at Three Oaks, where his wife now lived. "Of course, Mary Lou wouldn't be able to join in the workshops, but lots of the other residents would. Three Oaks offers classes all the time, and I know there are a number of talented seamstresses living there, and they'd love to take a specialized class. *Seamstresses* being a misleading word, by the way, since a number of those people are men," Mr. Willet added. "Anyway, what do you think?" he asked Min and Gigi, who had now joined Mr. Willet at the front of the store.

"It's a wonderful idea, Bill," said Gigi. "The only problem is that Min and I don't often leave the store at the same time."

"I have a thought, though," said Min. "What if Flora and I taught the classes?"

"Me?" cried Flora.

"You're capable," said Min.

"More than capable, I imagine," said Mr. Willet. "Well, I think that sounds fine. I'll talk to the activities director at Three Oaks and let you know what happens."

"Hey, Mr. Willet," said Ruby, "have you heard about Nelson Day?"

"Is that the fund-raiser to help the Nelson family?"

"Yup." Ruby nodded. "And it was all my idea." She glanced at Min. "But, um, it isn't just about me. I mean, everyone is helping with the project. Nearly everyone in town! You know," she went on, "I just thought of something. We're kind of like the animals in *The Rats of NIMH*, all doing our part for," she paused, "for one great cause."

"It sounds as though you girls are enjoying your secret book club," said Mr. Willet.

Olivia frowned. "You know about the book club? Did we mention it to you?"

"I think Min did," said Mr. Willet quickly.

The bell over the door jangled then. Min and Gigi got to their feet to help the customer, and Flora forgot about books and the book club and turned her attention to the thought of teaching a sewing workshop for grown-ups.

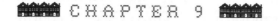 

# CHAPTER 9

# A Very Important Person

Mary Lou Willet's mind had once been sharp and clear. People had said she had an unusually good memory. Long ago, when she was a little girl, her second-grade teacher had told her mother that Mary Lou had a mind like a steel trap. Mrs. Willet was nearly seventy-nine now and her memory was fuzzy and fading. Worse, many everyday things no longer made sense to her.

"How *strange*," she would say when a tray of food was placed before her on the dining table.

"How *strange*," she would say when the television in the lounge was turned on and a performer began to sing.

"How *strange*," she would say when that man who might be her husband came to visit and brought with him news from a place he called Aiken Avenue.

It was because Mary Lou's mind had begun to fail

that Bill Willet, her husband, had finally made the decision to move her to Three Oaks, a continuing care retirement community featuring apartments for people who could live independently, rooms for people who needed nursing or special care, and a wing for people with Alzheimer's — people such as Mary Lou Willet, whose mind now took alarming turns down unfamiliar pathways and retrieved distorted information for her. "How *strange*."

Bill Willet felt remarkably lucky to have secured a room for Mary Lou at Three Oaks so quickly.

It was because of the Willets that Nikki Sherman knew of the good reputation of Three Oaks. So when Mrs. Sherman returned from work one evening and announced that she had applied for a job as the dining supervisor there, Nikki was pleased.

"It's a big job," Mrs. Sherman added, "a full-time job."

"What you've been looking for!" exclaimed Mae, who was listening from her place at the kitchen table.

Mrs. Sherman smiled. "Yes, it is. It would mean a lot of changes for us, though. I'd have to leave every morning before eight, and I wouldn't get home until after six in the evening. And sometimes I'd have to work on weekends or holidays." (Nikki wrinkled her nose.) "On the other hand," Mrs. Sherman continued, "the salary is great. More money than I earn at my part-time jobs put together."

"Would we be rich?" asked Mae rapturously.

"No. But we'd be in much better shape."

"When will you find out if you have the job?" Tobias wanted to know.

"Next Friday. I was asked to come in for an interview — I went on my lunch break today — and the woman I talked with said she'd have an answer next Friday."

Today was that Friday, and Nikki's nerves were in a tangle as she waited for her mother to return at the end of the day with news.

"What if she doesn't *have* any news?" Nikki said peevishly to Tobias at breakfast. "What if the woman at Three Oaks hasn't made up her mind after all?"

Tobias shrugged. "Then we wait a little longer."

"I don't see how you can be so calm about this. . . . I'm going to call Mom this afternoon to see if she's heard anything."

"At the restaurant? Don't call her there," said Tobias. "Really, don't. You know how they are about personal phone calls. And if Mom doesn't get the new job, then she's going to want to hold on to her old ones."

Nikki sighed. "Won't it be great not to have to worry about money all the time?"

"Yup. And I won't have to worry about you and Mom and Mae so much."

"What do you mean?" asked Nikki.

"When I'm away at school. I mean, *if* I go away."

"Tobias! Did you decide to go?"

"Pretty much."

"Why didn't you say anything?"

"Because I'm still thinking about it. But . . . I guess I know what I'm going to do. I just haven't done it yet."

"Wow," said Nikki. "College. I've dreamed about it since I was Mae's age. And now you're going to get to go. You are so lucky."

"I know. But you'll go, too, Nikki. You're a much better student than I am. Talented, too. You have your art. You'll get a scholarship for sure."

"I can't believe you'll be leaving. Mom and Mae and I will be here by ourselves. That'll be weird. Just the three of us."

"I know."

"I won't be scared, though," said Nikki, who, even as she spoke the words, was thinking that she might in fact be quite scared. "Bad things don't usually happen in Camden Falls."

"Well, don't get . . . what's the word?"

"Complacent?" suggested Nikki.

"See?" said her brother. "I'm the one going to college, and you're the one who knows words like *complacent*. Trust me, seven years from now, you'll be off to college, too. It will happen somehow. The old bat — I mean, Mrs. DuVane — will help you." Mrs. DuVane, a wealthy acquaintance of Nikki's mother, had years earlier, in a blunt and tactless way, taken on the Shermans as what had felt to Nikki and her family like something of a charity project. But over time, she had softened, and Nikki had been grateful for her many kindnesses.

"By then we might not need Mrs. DuVane anymore," said Nikki. "Won't need her money, anyway. If Mom gets the job, we could be on our feet seven years from now." She sighed. "Seven years. That sounds like such a long time. Imagine me, going to college. I'll be practically an adult by then."

"Are you saying I'm not an adult yet?" asked Tobias.

Nikki laughed. "No. You're an adult."

"Getting back to being complacent, though . . . Seriously, Nikki, I know this is Camden Falls and all, but when I'm gone, you and Mom and Mae have to be careful about locking the house at night —"

"You mean, because we'll be three girls alone way out in the country?"

"Nikki."

"We're going to be careful. I promise."

"You'd better be. Because if you're not, I'm going to come home from school."

"Tobias, we can take care of ourselves."

"I know you can."

When Nikki imagined lying in her bed, though, in the darkened Sherman house, her brother miles and miles away, she felt an uncomfortable hollowness in her chest, the same hollowness she used to feel sitting alone on the school bus, separated from her laughing classmates by both inches and miles.

Nikki spent the long, lazy afternoon by herself, waiting for her mother to come home. Tobias had left for his part-time job and Mae was at day care. Nikki was unaccustomed to so much time alone. She took her copy of *Roll of Thunder* onto the stoop, squatted down, and leaned against the wall of her house, stretching her skinny legs in front of her. Paw-Paw joined her, curling onto his side and pressing his back hotly against Nikki's bare leg. Nikki couldn't bring herself to move him.

She opened the book. She had stopped reading the night before at the end of Chapter Nine, a very exciting point in the story. Nikki hadn't wanted to stop, but the book had kept slipping from her hands, and she had finally realized that, exciting as the story was, she had read the last paragraph three or four times. Reluctantly, she had turned off her reading lamp. Now she turned to the tenth chapter, marked with a piece of cream-colored cardboard on which Mae had written vertically, NIKKI/SISTER/BEST FREIND. The bookmark had been Mae's birthday present to Nikki.

Nikki read. And read and read. She reached the

last sentences of the book: *I cried for T.J. For T.J. and the land.*

Nikki felt her own tears falling, and Paw-Paw looked up at her in alarm, then struggled to his feet and licked Nikki's face.

"It's okay, Paw-Paw," said Nikki.

She sat motionless on the stoop and thought about what Flora had said the other day — that it wasn't okay to hate anyone. But Nikki had very strong negative feelings about quite a few characters in the book, Lillian Jean, for instance, and Mr. Granger, and about what they felt they could do to Cassie simply because she was black.

"There are a lot of hateful people in the world," Nikki said to Paw-Paw. "People who are full of hate, I mean." And maybe that was why, Nikki reflected, Flora had said it wasn't okay to hate people — because then you became one of the hateful ones.

It was all very complicated. Nikki was grateful that soon she would be able to discuss the book with her friends. She had a lot to say about it.

Nikki went into the kitchen, placed *Roll of Thunder* reverently on the table, and got a drink of water. She returned to the porch and stood for a few moments in the hot silence of the July afternoon, regarding the sky, regarding the dusty earth, regarding the pinpricks of light in the distance, sunshine reflecting off cars on the county road.

Her mind strayed from the complications of Cassie Logan's story to something simpler and much safer. "Paw-Paw," said Nikki, turning around and finding him sprawled on his back, tail sweeping the porch, "I'm going to make you a costume for Halloween this year." Paw-Paw, who had the patience of a saint, according to Mrs. Sherman, had allowed Nikki and Mae to dress him, variously, as Santa Claws, a princess, a cat, and even Baby New Year.

Nikki spent the next hour trying various articles of clothing on Paw-Paw, who remained sleepy throughout the ordeal. Her thoughts swarmed dizzily like bees around their hive. She imagined Paw-Paw going trick-or-treating with her and Mae in town. She thought of Cassie Logan on her long walk to the Great Faith Elementary and Secondary School with her brothers. She wondered, briefly, where her father was. She thought that perhaps Camden Falls should hold a costume parade for dogs in the fall.

When at last Nikki heard the sound of her mother's car in the lane, she jumped off the stoop, abandoning Paw-Paw, who was wearing a T-shirt and two pairs of lace-edged socks.

"Did you get the job? Did you get it?" called Nikki, running into the yard.

Mrs. Sherman climbed out of the car. She was grinning and carrying a bag of takeout food. Before she could answer, Mae burst from the backseat of the car and cried, "Mommy got the big job!"

"I knew it! I knew you would!" Nikki threw her arms around her mother.

"I called Three Oaks from work this afternoon," said Mrs. Sherman. "I got the good news, hung up the phone, and quit both my jobs."

Nikki stooped to Mae's level and whispered in her ear, "Come upstairs with me. I have an idea."

That night when the Shermans sat down to their meal of takeout food — a luxury on which they rarely splurged — Mrs. Sherman wore a badge made from pink construction paper proclaiming her a Very Important Person.

# CHAPTER 10

# Complicated

One Saturday night, several months before the start of this summer that was changing Olivia in subtle but noticeable ways, Olivia, Flora, Nikki, and Ruby had had a sleepover at Min's house. In the wee hours of the morning, as the girls were starting to fall asleep, Ruby had said, "If you guys could each have just one wish, what would it be?"

Olivia had said, "I'd wish for endless wishes."

Ruby had said, "I'd wish to be a millionaire."

Nikki had said, "I'd wish I could go to sleep."

And Flora had said, "I'd wish I weren't shy. If I weren't shy, everything would be different."

Now Olivia, sitting alone in her backyard on a humid July Saturday, remembered Flora's words and thought, If I weren't smart, everything would be different. Immediately, she realized that wasn't true. Even if she weren't so smart, she would still be tiny and uncoordinated and uninterested in clothes and iPods and sports and boys. And she would still have been left off Tanya's guest list. Furthermore, she could understand Flora's wish not to be shy, but Olivia could never wish not to be smart. She thought the thrill she felt when she solved a tough problem to be akin to a bird soaring far above the earth and seeing everything clearly laid out below, like a puzzle that's already been pieced together. Olivia would never relinquish that clarity. But she still wondered how she might have felt if she had reached her hand into her mailbox and pulled out an invitation of her own.

Well, that moment was over, Olivia admonished herself. Over and done with and gone. And the summer was slipping by. Did she really want to face her first day back at school having moped away the entire vacation? No. And did she want to continue to punish Nikki and Flora for having gone to Tanya's party without her? No. Particularly not when she was the one who had urged them to go in the first place.

Olivia heard a small noise at the edge of her yard. She shook herself free of her thoughts and saw Ruby, Flora, and Nikki, each holding her copy of *Roll of Thunder*, crossing quietly from Min's yard into hers. Their approach was tentative, and Olivia knew why.

She felt a tickle of annoyance, followed by a tickle of regret. She stood up and called cheerfully, "Hey, you guys! Come look at our garden!"

Flora glanced at Nikki, then grinned and began to run. "Do we have any vegetables yet?" she called.

"Well, no, not yet," replied Olivia. "But everything is doing really well. Except for the cucumbers. Look at them." Olivia pointed to two plants that were now nothing but stalks, the leaves having been eaten away.

"What happened to them?" cried Ruby, sounding greatly affronted.

"Slugs. At least that's what Mr. Pennington said."

"Dang old slugs," said Ruby.

Olivia stood facing her friends, smiling at Ruby, and tried to figure out how to explain her complicated feelings to them. But she couldn't, at least not right away, so she was grateful when Nikki said, "I've been waiting and waiting to talk to you guys about the book."

"Me, too," said Ruby. "And before anyone asks, yes, I finished it." She didn't add that she had finished it ten minutes before Nikki had arrived that morning.

"Where do we start?" asked Flora. "There's so *much* to talk about."

Olivia sat in the grass at the edge of the vegetable garden, and the others sat with her.

"I want to start by apologizing," said Ruby.

"For what?" asked Nikki.

"For what I said about the Jim Crow laws. How could I ever have thought they sounded funny?"

"You didn't know," said Olivia. "You don't have to apologize. You'd only have to apologize if you still thought they were funny."

Ruby let out a yelp. "No! Now I see what you were saying about separate but equal, Olivia."

"And how it was really separate *and un*equal," said Nikki. "Like the schools."

"And their books," spoke up Flora. "I kept looking at the chart that was inside Little Man's reading book. There were so many things to notice about it — that when the book was eleven years old and judged to be in Very Poor condition, it was then given to a black student instead of a white student. The black students got all the old, ratty things."

"And the black students weren't called black or Negro," said Nikki. "They were called nigra."

"Did you notice," said Olivia, "that the word *White* was capitalized, but *nigra* wasn't? It didn't even deserve a capital letter."

"I wonder why the teacher, Miss Crocker, wasn't upset about the books," said Ruby. "I didn't understand that."

"I think that's what slavery did to people," said Flora.

"Slavery! The Logans weren't slaves. Miss Crocker wasn't a slave," said Ruby. "I thought this story took place years and years after slavery."

"It did. But it kind of felt to me like slavery hadn't ended. The effects still lingered."

"That's one of the things that make the story so complicated," said Olivia. "I mean, not the story itself, but the things that led to it."

"The things that led to the story having to be told," said Nikki.

Olivia consulted the letter that had accompanied *Roll of Thunder, Hear My Cry*. "I think I know now why we're supposed to talk about the Underground Railroad," she said.

"What *is* the Underground Railroad?" asked Ruby. "I never found anything about that in the book. Is it like a subway?"

"No," said Olivia, "it wasn't a railroad at all."

"It was a way for slaves to escape to freedom in the northern states or Canada or Mexico," explained Nikki.

"To escape secretly," added Flora. "People who were against slavery would help them travel at night, then take them to places where they could hide safely during the day."

"And you can see," said Olivia, "after you read about Mr. Granger and some of the other characters in the book, why slaves would have to escape like that. They would never have been allowed to go free otherwise. Even after abolition, lots of white landowners thought they had a right to use black people, to make them work for them. They just figured out other ways to get what they wanted."

The girls sat quietly for a few moments, and Olivia became aware of a pair of barn swallows chattering to each other in a tree in Mr. Pennington's yard.

"Why, I wonder," said Ruby finally, "didn't Cassie's family go north to escape Mr. Granger and all the trouble?"

"Because of the land," Olivia replied.

Ruby frowned. "What?"

"The land. *Their* land. Four hundred acres," said Olivia. "Cassie's grandfather had bought it fair and square. From the Grangers, no less. But it wasn't just that it had been Granger land. It was what the land represented."

"Freedom," said Nikki.

"Independence," said Flora.

"But now they couldn't afford the land," said Ruby, frowning again. "Cassie's father had to work on the railroad to earn extra money. Plus, there was so much trouble around. The burnings and beatings . . ."

"The Logans didn't want to run away," said Olivia.

"That's what I thought," said Flora. "And you know what I started remembering? *The Diary of Anne Frank*. Did any of you read that?"

"I did," said Nikki.

"I saw the movie," said Olivia.

"What is it?" asked Ruby.

"It's a true story," Flora began to say.

"Well, it actually *is* Anne Frank's diary," said Nikki.

"Anne Frank was a Jewish girl living in Amsterdam during the Second World War," Flora continued. "Her family saw trouble coming, but they couldn't leave, even though some other Jewish people were able to escape to safe countries. So the Franks lived in hiding in Amsterdam for two years, and Anne kept a diary during that time. Eventually, someone betrayed the Franks, and the Nazis came and took them all to concentration camps. Everyone in Anne's family died, except her father."

Ruby looked stricken. "But . . . but . . . that's *horrible*." She glared at the others. Then she said defiantly, "I would have found a way to leave Amsterdam. And I think the Logans should leave the South. That's what our last chapter should be about."

Flora regarded her sister. Finally, she said, "Ruby, if we started noticing trouble of some sort around here — just very subtle things at first — like maybe we hear that over in Bolton someone is beaten up because he speaks out in favor of something other people don't believe is right —"

"Like what?" said Ruby.

"I don't know. Like he says it's okay to hire people based on the color of their skin, and to refuse jobs to qualified African-Americans."

"But that's *wrong*," said Ruby.

"He has a right to his opinion, though, doesn't he? Anyway," said Flora, "let's say this man gets beaten up. Then someone gets beaten up for *supporting* fair hiring practices. And then in West Hook a store is burned down because the people who own it had put a sign in the window stating their feelings about equal rights. And then we start hearing rumors that this trouble is just going to keep growing and growing in a very frightening way, and that a lot of people are going to be in danger — like the Franks were. And *then* Min says we should escape to Canada. I mean, move there. What would you think, Ruby? Would you want to leave Camden Falls? Leave the Row Houses? Leave all our friends?"

"No," said Ruby in a small voice. "But how would we know this trouble was really going to grow? Maybe it would just go away."

"Maybe that's what the Logans hoped would happen in the South," added Olivia. "After all, slavery *had* ended years before. Things should have been getting better."

"I wonder why people like Mr. Granger were allowed to get away with the things they did to black people," said Nikki.

"It's so complicated," said Ruby.

"But it shouldn't be either complicated or simple," said Olivia, "because the things that led up to *Roll of Thunder* should never have happened in the first place. And they wouldn't have happened if people treated each other with kindness and fairness, instead of thinking they could own them and then step all over them and belittle them, too."

An uncomfortable silence followed, during which Flora looked at her watch. "Wow," she said softly. "We should really start writing our chapter. In exactly two and a half hours, we have to leave for the next part of our adventure."

"I'll go get my computer," said Olivia, jumping to her feet.

"I'm hungry!" exclaimed Nikki.

"Me, too," said Ruby, and the solemn mood was broken.

Olivia made four cheese sandwiches and brought them, along with four glasses of water and her laptop computer, to the Walters' picnic table.

"How long do you think a chapter should be?" asked Ruby, her mouth full of cheese.

"Any length," said Nikki.

"Whatever it takes to say what you want to say," added Flora.

Ruby scrunched up her face. "What are we going to say?"

"Do you still believe the Logans should move north?" asked Olivia.

Ruby looked absently at the backyards of the other Row Houses. "No."

"Let's think about the characters, then," said Nikki, "like the letter suggests. And let's start with T.J."

"T.J.!" cried Ruby. "What about Cassie? It's her story."

"But T.J. is mentioned in the very last sentence of the book," Nikki pointed out.

"Let's mention T.J., everyone in Cassie's family, and Mr. Morrison, since he was the Logans' friend," said Olivia.

"What about the mean characters?" asked Flora.

"Let's make bad things happen to them," said Ruby. "Put them all in jail. Even Lillian Jean."

Olivia laughed. "This is going to be some chapter," she said, and the girls set to work.

They were just finishing (Ruby had taken the computer from Olivia and was writing THE END in enormous purple capital letters), when Flora once again looked at her watch. This time she said, "Hey, we have to leave! Shut down the computer, Olivia."

Five minutes later, Olivia, Nikki, Ruby, and Flora set out for 357 Harmony Lane.

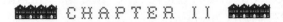 

# CHAPTER II

# The Secret Room

Flora opened the Walters' back door, and she and Olivia, Nikki, and Ruby hurried through the house and out the front door.

"Okay. Lead the way, Olivia," said Flora. "You're the only one who knows how to get to Harmony Lane."

With Olivia in charge, the girls headed north on Aiken Avenue.

"And now we make a left here," said Olivia.

"Well, this *is* exciting," exclaimed Ruby. "More like the Melendys' adventures. I've never been on this street before."

Flora studied the homes they were passing. "These houses look *really* old," she said. "Older than the Row Houses."

"They are," said Olivia. "I think some of them are two or three hundred years old."

"Wow," Nikki said breathlessly. "Imagine living back then, in colonial times."

"No electricity," said Ruby.

"No running water," said Olivia.

"You'd have to use an outhouse," said Flora, wrinkling her nose.

The girls reached another corner and Olivia said, "Turn right. This is Harmony Lane."

"It looks just like any other street," said Ruby, sounding puzzled.

"Well, it's not a *magic* street," Flora pointed out.

"Let me have my fantasies," Ruby replied.

Flora felt a fluttering in her stomach. "What do you suppose is going to happen when we get to number three fifty-seven?" she whispered.

"We're going to step back in time," Ruby intoned in a sepulchral voice.

"We're going to be swallowed whole by the house," said Nikki. "It's an evil house, like in a Stephen King book."

Flora shuddered.

"I wonder who lives at three fifty-seven," said Olivia.

"Don't you have any idea?" Ruby asked her.

"No! I would have said so already if I did." Olivia came to a halt. "But get ready to find out. This is the house."

Flora, feeling as nervous as if she were about to be

called on to give a report to her class, stopped and stared at the house before them. It rambled this way and that, reminding her of the Popsicle-stick structures she used to build, adding first one and then another and another room haphazardly, even after she had thought her house was finished.

"The house kind of wanders around," Ruby observed.

"It's pretty, though," said Olivia. "I like all the gardens."

"It looks like a house for gnomes!" exclaimed Nikki.

Flora laughed but said, "I'm a little afraid to ring the doorbell."

"We have to. Whoever lives here is expecting us," replied Olivia.

"All right. Let's be brave, then. Like Mrs. Frisby," said Flora.

"And the Logans," added Ruby.

The girls walked along a path to the house, clutching one another's hands. Flora was about to whisper, "Who's going to ring the bell?" when the door flew open and before them stood . . .

"Min!" cried Flora. "What are you doing here?"

Min smiled. "Visiting my friend Mrs. Angrim. This is her house."

A woman stepped from behind Min and beckoned to the girls. "Come inside," she said.

Flora, Ruby, Nikki, and Olivia walked through a doorway, the top of which was just inches above Min's head. Flora could easily have reached upward and gripped the door frame.

"Min," said Ruby eagerly, "are you —"

But Min interrupted her. "Helen," she said, turning to Mrs. Angrim, "meet my granddaughters. This is Ruby and this is Flora. And this," she continued, resting her hand on Olivia's shoulder, "is Olivia Walter. You know her grandmother. And this is Nikki Sherman."

"Hello, girls," said Mrs. Angrim. "I understand you've been talking about the Underground Railroad."

"That wasn't a real railroad, you know," said Ruby knowledgeably. "It wasn't even a subway."

Mrs. Angrim smiled. "No. I suppose you know what it was, then."

"Sort of," said Ruby.

"We studied it in school," said Olivia.

"Well, I was told you might like to see the basement of my house."

"The basem —" Ruby started to yelp, but she was silenced by Flora, who jammed her sandal into Ruby's ankle.

"It was once," Mrs. Angrim continued, "a stop on the Underground Railroad."

Flora saw Nikki raise her eyebrows.

"It *was?*" exclaimed Olivia.

"Yes. Over a hundred and fifty years ago. The house

was much smaller then. The families who have lived in it over the years have added on — and on and on. Follow me and I'll show you the room."

"The room?" asked Nikki. "Just one room?"

"Yes. Off the main part of the basement. It had to be a good hiding place," Mrs. Angrim explained. "Nothing that would call attention to itself."

The girls and Min followed Mrs. Angrim through a series of small rooms. Like a rabbit warren, thought Flora, who decided she might feel a bit claustrophobic if she had to live in this house.

Mrs. Angrim made her way through the tiny kitchen, the others behind her single file, and at last she reached a trapdoor in the floor of a hallway. She pulled at a ring and the door rose with a creak. "Now down these stairs," she said cheerfully.

Flora gazed after Mrs. Angrim, who descended into the hole via a dusty staircase. She saw only darkness and began to think of spiders and toads and lizards. "Um," she said, but Mrs. Angrim pulled at a string hanging from the ceiling below, and the basement was suddenly illuminated. Flora could see nothing moving on the dirt floor and let out the breath she'd been holding.

When at last everyone had gathered in the basement, Mrs. Angrim led them to a dark corner and began to feel along one wall.

"Years ago, this wall was hidden by a movable

shelf," she explained. "Anyone looking around the basement would have seen only a storage area."

Flora watched in fascination as a section of the wall resolved itself into a door, which Mrs. Angrim pushed inward. She picked up a flashlight from the floor and aimed it through the tiny doorway. "This," said Mrs. Angrim, "was where escaping slaves could hide."

"In *here*?" exclaimed Ruby. "I mean, no offense, but was this room any nicer when it was part of the Underground Railroad?"

Flora was too astonished by what she saw before her to take much notice of Ruby's thoughtless remark. The room that had opened before the girls was dank, windowless, and small — about half the size of Flora's bedroom, which wasn't very big itself. It smelled of earth and dampness and whatever creatures thrived belowground, out of the way of sunlight and fresh air.

Mrs. Angrim addressed Ruby. "Well," she said, "there was some furniture in the room, but that was about it. And remember, there was no electricity then, so this room would have been lit only by candles or oil lamps."

"Excuse me," said Ruby, "but where did the people go to the bathroom? They couldn't leave this room, could they?"

"They used chamber pots," replied Mrs. Angrim.

Ruby looked helplessly at Min, who whispered to her, "I'll explain later."

Mrs. Angrim said briskly, "Escaping slaves traveled by night, for the most part, and often by boat. They didn't stay long anywhere, but sometimes they were able to hide out for several days and rest before moving on."

"I wonder how many people stayed here altogether," said Olivia thoughtfully. "I mean, over the years."

Mrs. Angrim shook her head. "I don't know. But it could have been quite a few. There were probably entire families in here from time to time."

"Families!" cried Ruby. "You mean there were kids? Kid slaves?"

"Absolutely," said Min.

"Slave owners believed that they owned any children their slaves gave birth to as well as the slaves themselves," added Mrs. Angrim.

Ruby didn't reply.

From a corner of the room, Flora heard Nikki mutter, "*Owning* people."

"Imagine anyone having to hide out just to survive," said Flora after a moment. She turned to Min and Mrs. Angrim. "Before we came over here we were talking about Anne Frank and her family and how they hid in the Secret Annex."

"How did you get from *Roll of Thunder, Hear My Cry* to that subject?" asked Min.

"We were wondering whether the Logans — in the book —" Olivia added for Mrs. Angrim's benefit, "should have left the trouble in the South and moved north. And then we started talking about people who have to leave their homes, and about what happened to Jewish people who stayed in Amsterdam during World War Two."

"Ah," said Min.

Nikki was digging into the earthen floor with the toe of her sneaker. "Think of all the lives that might have been saved because of this little room," she said.

"It's kind of exciting, I guess," said Ruby, "but mostly . . . it must have been so scary."

Flora shivered.

"I suppose," said Min later, after Mrs. Angrim had closed the trapdoor to the basement and was leading the way through her house once again, "that this was a different sort of adventure than the ones the children had in *The Saturdays.*"

"I'll say," replied Ruby. "Those kids lived in New York City and got to go to the circus and to an opera house and stuff."

"But," said Olivia, "today was really, really interesting."

"It was thought," Min went on, "that your visit here would make for an unusual adventure."

What an interesting choice of words, Flora said to herself. Aloud she said, "Thank you for showing us the room, Mrs. Angrim."

"Yes, thank you," said Nikki and Olivia and Ruby.

The girls walked back down the path to Harmony Lane, leaving Min behind with Mrs. Angrim.

"Did you guys hear what Min said just now?" asked Flora when Mrs. Angrim's door was safely closed. "She said, '*It was thought* that your visit here would make for an unusual adventure.'"

"Yeah?" said Ruby, who might just as well have said, "So?"

"She knows who set up the book club!" exclaimed Flora.

"Of course she does," said Olivia. "So do my parents and Nikki's mom. We already figured that out. Min's being very careful not to give away any clues about that person, including whether it's a man or a woman. I'll bet Gigi knows who it is, too. And if she knows, then Poppy does. I have a feeling Mr. Pennington knows, too. And probably a bunch of other people."

"But what I think," Flora continued, "is that *Min* is the secret person. *That's* why she had to be so careful about what she said. And look, there she was at Mrs. Angrim's house today."

"That doesn't prove anything," said Nikki as the girls turned a corner. "Besides, if Min is the mystery person, how did she deliver the packages to Needle and Thread the first day? They were already there when you arrived at the store that morning."

"She could have arranged for someone else to deliver them," said Ruby. "To throw us off the track."

"Ooh. Tricky," said Olivia.

"I like a good mystery," proclaimed Flora. "It's not every day one comes your way. Unless you're Nancy Drew."

Ruby clasped her hands together and gazed thoughtfully into the distance. "I wonder what's going to happen next," she said.

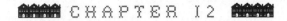 

# CHAPTER 12

# Robby's Bad Day

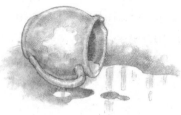

Three days a week, Robby Edwards worked as a clerk at Sincerely Yours. His shift started at ten in the morning, when either his mother or his father dropped him off at the store, and ended at three in the afternoon, when someone arrived to pick him up. In between, Robby waited on customers, stocked shelves, made coffee, and occasionally manned the cash register.

By the middle of July, Robby had been working for almost a month. He was pleased with the way his bank account was growing. But he was even more pleased by something that had happened the previous week: Olivia Walter had decided that four times a year, Sincerely Yours should honor a particularly hard-working employee and post that person's picture by the cash register. Robby had been selected as the Employee of the Summer.

"Dad! Dad!" he had cried when his father collected him that afternoon. "Look! I'm the Employee of the Summer! It says so right over there." He grabbed his father by the hand and tugged him inside the store. "See the sign? That makes it official."

"Robby, that's wonderful!" his father had exclaimed. And that night the Edwards family had celebrated with ice cream at Dutch Haus.

One sultry morning, when the July humidity had settled oppressively over Camden Falls, making Robby feel as if he were wearing a damp winter coat, Mr. Edwards walked along Main Street with his son.

"What does today hold for you?" he asked.

"Always the same," Robby replied with satisfaction. "First I will check the coffeepot, and if it is empty, I'll make more coffee. Then I'll straighten the merchandise. On the shelves. Maybe there will be new items to stock. But if any customers arrive and they need help, then I stop what I'm doing and help. The customers always come first."

Robby and his father passed Needle and Thread and peered through the windows. Gigi waved to them from the cutting counter. Robby waved back, then said, "Oh, there's Flora. She's going to teach a class, Dad. To *grown-ups*."

The Edwardses passed Zack's and Heaven and then they were standing outside Sincerely Yours. "Dad, don't hug me, okay?" Robby said urgently. "Tell me good-bye like a man."

Mr. Edwards looked gravely at his son. "Good-bye," he said. "Have a good day at work. This afternoon Margaret Malone is going to pick you up."

"Good-bye," replied Robby seriously. "You have a good day, too."

As Robby opened the door to Sincerely Yours he wished, as he often did, that he was allowed to walk to Main Street on his own. But then he reminded himself that he had a *job*. And he was earning a *paycheck*. He had already taken huge steps toward independence.

"Well! If it isn't the Employee of the Summer!" declared Mr. Walter, who was carrying a tray of cookies that Mrs. Walter had just made.

"I'm ready to check the coffee," was Robby's reply. He made his way to the coffee machine, reached for one of the pots, and knocked over a newly filled pot of milk. "Uh-oh! Uh-oh!" exclaimed Robby as milk pooled on the counter and dripped to the floor.

"Never mind," said Mrs. Walter. She bustled out of the kitchen with a dish towel and handed it to him.

Wordlessly, Robby cleaned up the mess. "Sorry, I'm sorry," he muttered when he had finished, and a memory flashed through his mind, quick as a snake, the memory of another summer day and of a girl — had she been a friend of Lydia Malone's? — whispering loudly that he was a retard.

This day, this stifling day when people in Camden Falls hustled from one air-conditioned building to another and complained about the heat in between, turned out to be a very bad day for Robby Edwards. He became confused when making change for a customer (before Robby had finished the transaction, the customer had handed him a ten-dollar bill and asked if Robby could give him a five and five ones, and also use one of the ones to buy a chocolate-chip cookie), and he was forced to call on Mr. Walter for help. Later, he was hauling a box of wooden picture frames to a display shelf, and just as he reached the shelf, the bottom of the box gave way and forty frames crashed to the floor, the glass in two of them breaking.

"Emergency!" Robby cried, horrified.

"Don't worry. Accidents happen," said Mrs. Walter. "That wasn't your fault."

And Mr. Walter added, "At least it wasn't a box of those." He pointed to a selection of expensive hand-painted glass ornaments that had recently arrived.

Robby tried to smile, but as he tackled the shards of glass with a dustpan and broom, he had the feeling that people walking by the store at that moment would see him and think, Retard.

"Time for your lunch break," said Mr. Walter gently when the mess had been cleared up. "Go relax for a while."

Humiliated, Robby ate a solitary lunch in the kitchen. The Walters were too busy to join him, and Robby was relieved. He used the quiet time to have a talk with himself, pointing out that it had just been a bad morning, and that when his lunch break was over, he could start fresh and try to pretend that the events of the morning hadn't taken place.

When Robby emerged from the kitchen, he found that Sincerely Yours was as crowded as he'd ever seen it.

"Everyone's escaping from the heat," he overheard Mrs. Walter say.

Without being told, Robby began to answer customers' questions. He directed them to new merchandise. He told Mrs. Walter when the chocolates in the candy counter were running low. When he noticed that no one was manning the cash register, he took it over. He rang up purchases and made change for nearly half an hour — without needing any help whatsoever.

His shift was almost over, the store still crowded, when a young man approached the cash register, reached into a Sincerely Yours shopping bag he was carrying, and removed the tissue paper that was protecting a glass rosebud. "Excuse me," he said to Robby, "I bought this this morning" (he pointed first to the rosebud and then to the display of painted ornaments) "and, well, my wife said it was too expensive and that I have to return it." He laughed uncomfortably.

Robby, peering at the display, saw that sure enough, one of the ornaments was missing. "Okay," said Robby.

"So do you think I could have my money back? All the ornaments are the same price, I'm pretty sure. The total came to eighty-five dollars even."

"Okay," said Robby again. He placed the ornament carefully on a shelf below the cash register, then opened the drawer, withdrew four twenty-dollar bills and one five, and handed them to the customer.

"Thank you, sir," said the man solemnly, and he left the store.

Robby carried the ornament back to the shelf and placed it in the empty spot between a glass bell and a glass bird.

"Was someone interested in that?" asked Mr. Walter.

"The man who bought it this morning returned it," Robby answered. "I gave him his money back."

Mr. Walter pursed his lips. "I don't remember selling one of those. I don't think we've sold any of them yet. Did the customer show you his receipt?"

Robby's gaze traveled to the floor. "No. But he had the ornament. He returned it," he said again. "In one of our shopping bags."

"Wendy?" Mr. Walter called. "Did you sell one of the new ornaments today?"

"No," Mrs. Walter called back.

Mr. Walter sighed. "Robby," he said, "I think we've been tricked. I think that man probably stole the ornament, then said he had to return it. That's why we always need a receipt when someone wants his money back or wants to exchange something."

Robby felt his face burning. "Oh."

"Don't worry," said Mr. Walter. "Everyone makes mistakes."

But I make more than most people, thought Robby. He looked out the window, then back at Mr. Walter. "I just cost you eighty-five dollars," he said. "You can take it out of my pay."

"What?" said Mrs. Walter from across the store. She joined Robby and her husband. "Why are we taking something out of your pay?"

Mr. Walter explained what had happened.

"And I want to pay you back," said Robby miserably.

"Absolutely not," said Mrs. Walter. "We won't hear of it."

"Thank you," mumbled Robby. He glanced at the door. "Margaret's here," he said. "I have to go."

Robby made his way to Margaret Malone. As he passed the checkout counter, he snatched the Employee of the Summer sign from the cash register and crumpled it into a tight ball. Moments later, he tossed it in a garbage can on Main Street.

CHAPTER 13 image

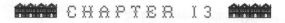

# Nikki Sherman, Private Investigator

The heat in Camden Falls was unrelenting that July, and Nikki, whose house had no air-conditioning, spent a great deal of time in town with Olivia, Ruby, and Flora. Sincerely Yours was air-conditioned, Needle and Thread was air-conditioned, the Row Houses were air-conditioned. And Min and the Walters were allowing the girls to stay at home alone more and more often.

"A good thing, too," said Olivia, "since I want to start baby-sitting for Grace. I wonder when the Fongs will decide I'm old enough to do that."

Nikki regarded Olivia, grateful that her old friend seemed to have returned. She had no idea why, but ever since the day of their last Saturday adventure, the day they had visited Mrs. Angrim's house, Olivia had been her sunny, bouncy self — as long as no one mentioned

117

Tanya, her party, barbecues, swimming pools, or Camden Falls Central High School.

"Have you ever taken care of a baby before?" Nikki asked.

She and Flora were sitting on Olivia's bed, watching Olivia remove every article of clothing from the wardrobe in the corner of her room. Olivia was growing (much to her relief), and her mother had told her it was time to try on all of her clothes in order to weed out the ones that no longer fit. When that chore had been accomplished, they would go shopping for new clothes.

"Well," Olivia replied, "I helped take care of Henry and Jack when they were babies."

"I don't know if that counts," said Flora.

Olivia tossed a shirt onto a pile in the middle of the room. She had barely been able to squeeze her head through the neck hole. "This is boring," she said, but she reached for another shirt. "You know what? We should be getting our next book any day now."

"I was just thinking the same thing!" exclaimed Nikki. "Also . . . I was getting an idea."

"You look awfully sneaky," observed Flora.

"Wait until you hear my idea. Okay, did you guys notice that both times we got books, they arrived on the same day of the week?"

"Yes," said Olivia and Flora.

"And that they arrived early in the morning?"

"Yes."

"Well, if my calculations are right —"

Olivia let out a laugh.

"Ahem," said Nikki. "If they're right, then the next packages should come in three days."

Flora jumped to her feet, peered at the calendar on Olivia's wall, and said, "I'll bet you *are* right!"

"So here's my sneaky idea," Nikki continued. "You know how the packages were left at Needle and Thread before it opened? Well, what if, three days from now, we went into town really early in the morning and hid somewhere nearby so we could see who leaves the envelopes?"

"Ooh," said Olivia. "That *is* sneaky. Except I don't think Mom and Dad will let me do that."

"I *know* Min won't let Ruby and me do that," said Flora.

Nikki frowned thoughtfully. "Okay. How about if *I* go into town?"

"All by yourself?" said Olivia.

"If I have to."

"Will your mother let you?" asked Flora.

"She won't know anything about it. She's already started her new job. She leaves the house before eight o'clock. And she takes Mae with her so she can drop her at day care. Tobias sleeps late — the whole house could fall on him and he wouldn't wake up. I figure if I'm ready to go when Mom leaves, I can get on my bike the moment her car is out of sight and be on Main Street by eight-fifteen. That's forty-five minutes before Needle and Thread opens. Maybe I'll catch the mystery person in the act."

"Ooh, I like this idea," said Olivia. "Where are you going to spy from?"

"That's a good question. I have to be able to see Needle and Thread, but I don't want to be out in the open. I don't want anyone to see *me*."

"I hate to suggest this," said Olivia, "but what if you hid across the street in the doorway of Stuff 'n' Nonsense? You'd be out of sight, and you'd have a great view of Needle and Thread."

"Stuff 'n' *Nonsense*?" cried Nikki. "The *Grinch's* store?" Nikki and Mrs. Grindle had a sorry history stemming from the previous summer when Mrs. Grindle had accused the innocent Nikki of stealing a necklace from her store.

"She won't be there at that hour," Olivia pointed out. "Stuff 'n' Nonsense doesn't open until ten that day. She'll never know."

"Hmm." Nikki paused thoughtfully. "I kind of like the idea of using Mrs. Grindle to further our cause. Okay, let's make plans."

Three days later, Nikki Sherman was awake and dressed by seven-thirty.

"Goodness, you're up early," said her mother.

Nikki shrugged. "I don't want to waste any of the summer."

Mrs. Sherman eyed her but said nothing.

"So how's the job?" asked Nikki.

Mrs. Sherman smiled. "It's wonderful. It's *really* wonderful. I know the hours are long and that that isn't easy on you and Tobias and Mae. But I love working at Three Oaks. Everyone there is so nice. My co-workers, the residents."

"That's great, Mom," replied Nikki seriously. "I never heard you say that about any of your other jobs."

Half an hour later, Mrs. Sherman's car was disappearing down the drive, and Nikki, having peeked into Tobias's room to make sure he was sound asleep (he was), was unlocking her bicycle. Fifteen minutes after that, following one of her fastest rides ever into Camden Falls, Nikki relocked her bicycle at a rack in front of the library, looking over her shoulder all the while. Main Street was quiet, though, and Olivia had been right: Stuff 'n' Nonsense wouldn't open until ten. Relieved, Nikki ducked into the doorway, trained her eyes across the street — and saw that four thick envelopes were already stacked by the entrance to Needle and Thread.

"No way," said Nikki under her breath.

She slouched away from Stuff 'n' Nonsense, hands in her pockets.

It was now eight-twenty. Nikki had half an hour to kill before Flora, Olivia, and Ruby would arrive at Needle and Thread with Min. She set off down Main Street, a very different place at this early morning hour. Nikki saw that she was one of just a handful of people in town. She watched as a teenage boy, with lank brown hair falling across his eyes and jeans falling well below his waistline, unlocked the door of the T-shirt Emporium. Across the street, Zack was letting himself into the hardware store. Farther down the block, a customer hurried into the post office, which, Nikki knew, Jackie and Donna had opened at precisely eight o'clock.

Nikki ambled along the sidewalk in the direction of Boiceville Road. In the windows of many of the storefronts, she saw signs advertising Nelson Day, the fund-raiser to help the Nelson family. She paused to read one of the signs. Nelson Day — which would feature a street fair with sidewalk sales, food, and music — would take place on Labor Day, which was also the end of summer vacation. And then . . . and then Nikki, Olivia, and Flora would officially become students at Camden Falls Central High School. They would be members of the youngest class, in there with all the older kids, kids as old as eighteen. Nikki shivered despite the heat that was gathering. Olivia wasn't the only one who was nervous about September.

Nikki shook herself and opened the door to Frank's Beans. After checking her pockets, she stepped up to the counter, greeted Frank, and, feeling extraordinarily grown-up, ordered an iced tea with extra ice. She selected a seat facing Main Street and sat by the window, sipping her drink, until she saw Min, Olivia, Ruby, and Flora approaching Needle and Thread. In a flash, Nikki tossed her cup in the trash and ran out the door. But she slowed down after she crossed the street. The plan was for Nikki to saunter down the sidewalk and pretend, for Min's sake, that she had just arrived in town.

"Hi!" she called to her friends.

Min was unlocking the door. "Hello, Nikki," she said. "I didn't expect to see you so early."

Ruby held out the packages. "Look what's *here!*" she cried. "What a sur*prise!* Did *any*body have *any* idea it was time for the next books to arrive? And what a co*in*cidence — we're all here to open them."

Olivia poked Ruby. "Tone it down, tone it down," she murmured.

Ruby scowled, but Nikki said brightly, "I can't wait to see what we got."

Min held the door open for the girls, and they rushed inside with the packages.

"Who brought them?" whispered Ruby loudly as soon as Min was behind the checkout counter.

"*SHHH!*" hissed Flora. "Min's already suspicious

♡ **123** ♡

because Olivia wanted to come with us this morning."

"I don't care!" exclaimed Ruby. "Who brought them?"

"I didn't see," confessed Nikki. "I got here at eight-fifteen — as soon as I could — and the packages were already in the doorway. Someone must have left them overnight, or else really, *really* early this morning."

"Dang," said Olivia.

"Oh, well. Let's open them," said Flora. "I don't care if the mystery person is still a mystery. It's more fun that way."

Nikki and her friends sat on the couches, each holding her package. "One, two, three . . . open!" cried Nikki.

Olivia was the first to withdraw the book. "*The Summer of the Swans*, by Betsy Byars," she said. She flipped through it. "It's short."

"It has pictures, just like *Mrs. Frisby and the Rats of NIMH*," commented Ruby approvingly.

"You know what?" said Flora. "This book won the Newbery Medal, and so did *Roll of Thunder* and *Mrs. Frisby*."

"What's the Newbery Medal?" asked Ruby.

"It says right on the book. It's an award for 'the most distinguished contribution to American literature for children.'"

"Cool," said Olivia.

"Let's read the letter," said Nikki. She unfolded hers and after a moment said, "Guess what the Saturday activity is. We're supposed to hold a Brave Saturday and each do something brave. I wonder why."

"I guess we'll know after we read the book," said Flora.

"Let's read it right now!" cried Olivia.

"What — the whole thing?" asked Ruby.

"Sure. Why not? It's short. I'll bet we could finish it in a few hours. Does anybody have anything else to do today? We could go right across the street to the library and read in those comfy chairs."

"Okay. Let me just call Tobias and tell him where I'll be," said Nikki.

It was not often that Nikki spent an entire day on Main Street, but on that sticky July day she didn't return home until nearly suppertime. After she and her friends read *The Summer of the Swans* (the older girls entertained themselves on a computer while they waited for Ruby to read the last several chapters), they left the library for College Pizza, where they sat at a booth and ordered sodas.

"Now I see why we're going to have Brave Saturday," said Nikki. "All the books we've read so far, except maybe *The Saturdays*, are about bravery."

*The Summer of the Swans* was the story of Sara Godfrey, who spends a night in the woods searching for her little brother, Charlie, after he disappears trying to find six swans that have shown up that summer.

"Does Charlie have the same thing Robby does?" asked Ruby as they waited for their sodas.

Olivia shook her head. "Robby has Down syndrome. And Charlie — I don't know. He doesn't talk."

"The kids are mean to him," said Ruby.

"The kids are mean to Sara, too," Nikki pointed out, "because her family is different and they don't have much money. I know exactly how Sara feels. I know a little how Cassie feels in *Roll of Thunder*, too. Outcasts."

"Things are better for you now, though, aren't they?" asked Flora anxiously.

"Better," agreed Nikki. "But I think once you've felt that way, it stays with you."

"Probably we all feel like outcasts sometimes," said Olivia.

Nikki played with her straw paper, folding it back and forth, back and forth, into an accordion. Then she dripped water on it and watched it spring to life. No one spoke.

The waitress brought their sodas. When she had left, Ruby said, "Well, I don't know *what* I'm going to do on Brave Saturday. I'm not afraid of anything."

Flora snorted. "Everyone's afraid of something, Ruby."

"You're afraid of so many things, you'll have trouble choosing," Ruby retorted.

"Girls, girls. No fighting now," said Olivia in her best Gigi voice.

"Let's have Brave Saturday this Saturday," said Nikki.

"*This* Saturday?" exclaimed Olivia. "But that's so soon."

"Do you have anything else to do?" asked Flora.

"No," admitted Olivia.

"Well, okay then. Let's start thinking."

"I have an idea," said Ruby. "Let's keep our brave things secret until Saturday. We won't reveal them to each other until we're ready to do them."

"Remember," added Nikki, "the letter said we each have to do something *truly* brave."

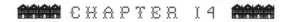 

# CHAPTER 14

# Brave Saturday

"How are we going to decide who goes first?" asked Ruby.

It was Saturday. To be more exact, it was the first Saturday of August, which was the month in which Ruby would begin her Turbo Tappers class, the month in which the girls' garden would finally begin producing vegetables, and the last month of summer vacation.

It was also Brave Saturday, and Ruby and her sister and friends were sitting in the shade of a beech tree in Min's backyard. Daisy Dear, who had been resting beneath a lawn chair, front legs stretched daintily before her, now crawled out from under the chair, padded across the lawn to the girls, and lowered herself to the grass at Ruby's feet. Her sides were heaving and she was panting, her mouth open wide.

"Daisy looks like she's smiling," observed Olivia.

"She's just as happy as we are to be outside," Flora replied. "Even if she is hot. I asked her two times if she wanted to go indoors, and she wouldn't budge. I think she's tired of being cooped up in the air-conditioning."

"Ahem," said Ruby. "I asked a question."

"Who will go first today?" said Nikki.

Ruby nodded.

"How about if we draw straws?" said Flora. She turned to Olivia and Nikki. "That's what our father used to suggest when we needed to make a choice," she explained.

"That won't work," objected Ruby. "We need a fifth person to hold the straws."

"Okay, then let's make four slips of paper," said Nikki, "and write a number — one, two, three, or four — on each slip. We'll put the slips in a bowl and each choose one. With our eyes closed. Whoever gets number one will go first and so on."

"Perfect!" said Ruby, who ran inside and returned with a piece of paper, a pencil, and a plastic mixing bowl. "Now," she said when the slips of paper were ready, "who gets to draw first?"

Olivia giggled. "This could go on forever. We'll all

draw them at the same time, okay? Everybody, close your eyes. On your mark, get set, go!"

After a brief scramble of hands in the bowl, Nikki said, "Does everybody have one?"

"Yes," said Olivia, Ruby, and Flora.

"Then open your eyes."

"Uh-oh," said Flora, peering at her piece of paper. "I guess I'm going first. Well, I'll be glad to get it over with. Who's going second?"

"Me," said Nikki.

"I'm going third," said Olivia.

"And I'm last," said Ruby. "Darn. I'll probably have to wait all day."

Three heads turned to Flora.

"So what are you going to do?" asked Olivia.

Flora drew in her breath. She let it out slowly and said, "I'm going . . . to hold a snake."

Ruby screamed.

"Cool," said Nikki.

"Where are you going to find a snake?" asked Olivia.

"At the Cheshire Cat. I'm sure Sharon will let me hold one." The Cheshire Cat, Camden Falls's pet store, sold pet supplies and small animals — but no cats or dogs, since, as Sharon the owner pointed out, there were already plenty of stray cats and dogs who needed homes.

"Is this *really* a brave thing you'll be doing?" Nikki asked Flora.

"Are you kidding?" said Flora, just as Ruby said, "For Flora it is."

"All right, then. Let's go."

The girls led Daisy Dear back into Min's house and then headed for Main Street. When they reached the Cheshire Cat, they stood in a row and looked through the window.

"Maybe they don't have snakes right now," said Ruby.

"Yes, they do. I already checked," replied Flora. "Little garden snakes or garter snakes. I can't remember. But some kind that doesn't bite. Not that it matters. I'm afraid of every single thing about a snake."

"I think you're going to be surprised when you actually hold one," said Olivia.

"What if it slithers out of my hand and escapes?"

"Then I'll catch it," replied Olivia. "Come on."

The girls entered the store, found Sharon, and told her about Brave Saturday.

"And so," said Flora, "I've decided that what I'm going to do is hold a snake, since I'm very, very afraid of them."

"You're sure about this?" asked Sharon, who was smiling.

"Positive. Unless you think it's mean to the snake or something."

"No, just be gentle."

Sharon reached into a cage and withdrew a small green snake. "Hold out both hands," she said.

Flora obliged, and Sharon laid the snake across them.

"*Aughhh!*" shrieked Flora, but she held still. The snake began to slide forward, and Flora moved her hands with it. "It's soft," she said after a moment. "It isn't slimy like I was expecting. It feels sort of silky." She paused. "How long do you think I've been holding it?"

"About ten seconds," said Nikki.

"That's enough."

Sharon took the snake back, and at once Flora began jumping up and down, wiping her hands on her shorts. "I did it! I did it!" She turned to Sharon. "Can I go wash my hands?"

Five minutes later, Flora, Ruby, Nikki, and Olivia were once again standing on Main Street. "Your turn," Ruby said to Nikki.

"Okay. Well . . . all I have to do is go to the post office."

"What for?" asked Olivia.

"I have to mail a letter. It's right here in my pocket." Nikki patted her jeans.

"That doesn't sound very brave," said Ruby.

"It's a letter to my father." Nikki looked sternly at Ruby. "And I'm not going to tell any of you what's in it. That's private." She kicked at a pebble. "At first I thought maybe my brave thing would be telling Mrs. Grindle, to her face, exactly how I felt last summer when she accused me — in public — of taking the necklace. But then I decided that that had happened too long ago. Anyway, just believe me, sending this letter to my dad is very brave. There are a few things I wanted to say to him."

A portion of the letter flashed through Nikki's memory: *I don't know if it's correct to say that you "abandoned" us, since you didn't love us. Don't you have to love a person in order to truly abandon her? I don't know. Maybe not. But anyway, you had a responsibility to us, and you chose to leave us. So now I think I have the right to tell you what kind of a father you were to me.* Nikki winced.

Olivia, Flora, and Ruby were quiet until finally Flora said, "You know where your father is, then?"

"Sort of. He writes to my mom from a post office box in a town in South Carolina. That doesn't necessarily mean he lives there. Mom thinks he lives somewhere nearby."

"Nikki," said Flora, "I know you don't want to tell us what you wrote, but I can sort of imagine. Are you sure you want to send the letter? I think it was pretty brave of you just to write down your feelings. Maybe you could leave it at that."

Nikki looked at her friends. "No," she said after a moment. "I mean, thank you, but I want to mail the letter. For me, that's the truly brave part. And I want to make absolutely sure the letter goes out. I'm not going to drop it in the mailbox. I want to hand it personally to Donna or Jackie."

The Cheshire Cat was located next to the post office. Nikki turned now to look through the post office window. Inside, she could see Donna and Jackie standing behind the counter, waiting on customers.

"Are you ready?" asked Olivia.

Nikki nodded. She pushed the door open and her friends followed her inside.

Nikki stepped up to the counter. "Hi, Donna," she said. "I have a very important letter here and I want to make *sure* it gets mailed. Can I give it to you instead of dropping it in the slot?"

"Absolutely," Donna replied seriously, and she held out her palm.

Nikki placed the letter on it. For a moment, she felt like jumping up and down and wiping her hands on her jeans, as Flora had done after handing the snake back to Sharon. Instead, she turned slowly from the counter and walked toward the door. She looked back at Donna once, and Donna said, frowning, "Are you certain you want to mail this?"

"Yes." Nikki walked out the door.

Ruby, Flora, and Olivia waited a few moments before following her.

"Nikki, are —" Flora started to say.

But Nikki cut her off. "Okay, Olivia. It's your turn now."

"Let's go sit on the benches," said Olivia, pointing across the street to the town square. "I have to explain something to you guys before I do my brave thing."

The girls found an empty bench by a water fountain and sat on it in a row.

Olivia, at one end, leaned forward so the others could see her. "All right. Here's the thing," she began. "This probably seems silly to you, but it isn't silly to me —"

"What isn't?" asked Ruby.

"I'm going to tell you! It probably seems silly to you," Olivia continued, "but I can't stop thinking about Tanya's party. You just don't know how much it hurts to be left out of something."

"I do," said Nikki.

Olivia nodded. "Maybe. But I was left out of something two of my best friends were invited to. That's mainly why I was so upset — I felt like I was being torn apart from you guys. And right before we move to the central school, where I think I'll need you more than ever. Plus, I feel like you two just got bumped up to something better — you know, socially — and I was left behind with the b —" Olivia, glancing at Ruby, caught herself before she said the word *babies*. "And I was left behind."

"But —" said Flora.

"Wait," said Olivia. "I know what you're going to say, or I think I do — that that would never happen, we're friends forever, blah, blah, blah. But I *still* felt left out. So . . . I made a decision: I'm going to give a party of my own. And I'm going to invite Tanya and the girls who went to her party, and you, too, Ruby. I just want to show Tanya that we can *all* be friends, that she doesn't have to leave me out. I already talked to Mom and Dad about this and they said I could have the party at Sincerely Yours. I have no idea how it's going to go. I don't know anything *about* parties, really. But I'm going to try this."

Olivia stood up then. "I have something in my pocket, too," she said, smiling at Nikki. "And we have to go back to the post office." Olivia reached into her pocket and pulled out a handful of envelopes. "The invitations," she said. "All ready to be mailed."

Ruby saw that Olivia's hands were shaking.

The girls crossed the street to the post office, and Olivia dropped the invitations in the mailbox by the door. "Oh, boy," said Olivia under her breath, and Flora squeezed her hand.

Flora, Olivia, and Nikki then turned to Ruby.

"Okay," Flora said, raising her eyebrows. "You're the last one."

Ruby was uncharacteristically quiet. Her face began to grow red.

"Come on. What is it, O Sister Without Fears?"

"Well," said Ruby, staring off down Main Street, "we have to go home. And we have to go to your room, Flora."

"Why —"

"No questions," said Ruby. "Let's just go."

So Ruby, Flora, Olivia, and Nikki walked back to Aiken Avenue, back to the Row Houses, and along the walk to the fourth one from the left. Ruby led the way upstairs. She stepped into Flora's room and said, "Where's Mom's diary?"

"Mom's diary?" Flora repeated. When Ruby didn't answer her, she opened the bottom drawer of her bureau and pulled out the notebook. "I keep it here now," she said.

Ruby reached for it. "I'm going to read this," she announced.

"I thought you didn't care about it," said Flora. She remembered the day she had discovered the old notebook in a dark recess of her wardrobe and realized it was a diary her mother had kept decades earlier. Flora had opened the notebook and begun to read it at once, but Ruby had seemed uninterested and hadn't asked to see it again.

"No," said Ruby quietly, "I never said that."

"I guess that's true," said Flora thoughtfully. She sat on the bed next to her sister. "What's this about, Ruby? Tell us."

"I didn't want to read the diary because . . . I thought it would hurt too much. I don't see how you can read it, Flora. You think you're not a brave person, but *I* think you do brave things all the time, and reading the diary is one of them. I can't imagine what it will feel like to see Mom's handwriting, and to hear her voice in the words, but I'm going to read the diary now. Some of it, anyway."

"Do you want us to leave you alone?" asked Flora.

Ruby hesitated. "Yes," she said.

Flora, Olivia, and Nikki edged toward the hallway. Flora almost asked Ruby whether she was sure about her decision, then changed her mind and closed the door quietly behind her, leaving Ruby curled on Flora's bed.

Ruby opened the notebook and found herself thrust into the twelfth year of her mother's life. She read about her mother's friends and her crushes on boys, about her longings and frustrations. She heard her mother's voice and found that she didn't feel sad after all; she felt comforted. Maybe this was why Flora turned so often to the diary.

Twenty minutes later, Ruby opened Flora's door

and found her sister and friends across the hall in her room. She joined them on the bed.

"Are you okay?" asked Flora.

The diary lay in Ruby's lap. "Can I keep this in my room for a while?" she asked.

Flora nodded. "We'll share it."

"Let's get something to eat," Ruby suggested.

"This has been a very thought-provoking day," said Olivia, stretching.

"I think it might be my favorite Saturday so far," added Nikki.

The girls stood up. They were making their way down the stairs to the kitchen when Flora suddenly shouted, "I held a snake!"

# CHAPTER 15

# *And Sew On and Sew Forth*

The first time Flora had visited Three Oaks was on a chilly, dreary day in December, and her impression of the retirement community, as Mr. Willet drove her, Ruby, Min, and Mr. Pennington past the buildings, had not been favorable. Three Oaks, she thought then, was a place of dull colors and blank walls.

"Remember the first time we came here?" Flora now asked Min as her grandmother circled the visitors' parking lot.

"I do," said Min.

"I didn't like it. Not at first."

"Neither did I."

"But then we went inside and everything was different."

"And we only saw one wing," Min reminded

**140**

her. "The wing Mary Lou was going to move to. We didn't even see the apartments where the other residents live."

"Min? Do we have time to visit Mrs. Willet before we start the class?"

Flora's grandmother glanced at her watch. "If it's a very quick visit, honey."

"Is Mr. Willet going to come to our class?"

"Yes. He's visiting Mary Lou now, but then he'll join us."

"Mr. Willet spends more and more time with Mrs. Willet, doesn't he?"

"He certainly does."

"How long have the Willets been married? Do you know?"

"Nearly sixty years."

"Sixty years!" exclaimed Flora. "How long were you married, Min?"

"A long time. But not as long as the Willets."

Min pulled into a parking space, and she and Flora climbed out of the car and opened the trunk. Flora eyed the carton she had stowed there. "I hope everyone likes the project we chose for our first class."

Min had come up with the idea of making glasses cases that could be embellished with embroidery, buttons, beads, or a combination of the three. "I hope so, too," she said. "I think it's a good first project because it will work for beginners or for people with more advanced skills."

Flora carried the box across the parking lot, following Min to the main building. The front door slid open automatically, and Flora and her grandmother found themselves in a cheerful, airy lobby with a reception desk and, next to it, a table on which sat a cage holding a small blue-and-white bird. On the wall beside the cage was a sign that read, HI, I'M WOODY THE THREE OAKS PARAKEET. PLEASE TALK TO ME, BUT DO NOT PUT YOUR FINGERS IN MY CAGE!

While Min spoke with the receptionist, Flora set the box on the floor and looked around the lobby. The room was large, with a high ceiling, in the middle of which was a skylight. Warm sun shone through the skylight, its rays enveloping the couches below in a soft glow. The lobby was quiet, except for Woody's twittering, and Flora felt a sense of calm.

A woman riding a motorized cart handed a sheaf of papers to the receptionist, then continued on her way. A man who reminded Flora of Mr. Willet walked by, talking earnestly to an elderly couple. "This is the main building," he was saying. "The pharmacy is down that way, and so is the wing for people with Alzheimer's. Over here is the coffee shop. Let's stop in and have a cup of tea."

Flora watched them walk toward a set of glass doors,

and she heard the woman say, "My goodness. They have *every*thing here, don't they?"

"Flora?" said Min. "Let's have a quick visit with Mary Lou. Mr. Willet is on his way to meet us. After we see Mary Lou, he'll take us to the activities room and we'll set up. You can leave the box here at the desk for now."

Moments later, a smiling Mr. Willet waved to Min and Flora as he strode through the hallway. "Hello there!" he said. "Everyone is very excited about the class. I know it's going to be wonderful. But come with me first. I'll take you to Mary Lou."

Flora saw Mrs. Willet long before Mrs. Willet realized she had visitors. She was sitting in a wheelchair on a shaded terrace with several other people, also in wheelchairs, most of them dozing in the heavy air.

"Mary Lou?" said Min, standing directly in front of her old friend. "Hi. It's Min Read. From the Row Houses. I brought Flora with me."

Slowly, Mary Lou Willet raised her head and focused her eyes on her visitors. But she didn't smile. Flora thought her face looked as if it were made of stone.

"It's Min and Flora," said Min again.

Flora noticed several stains on Mrs. Willet's blouse, a scattering of crumbs in her lap.

"FloraFloraFlora," said Mrs. Willet at last. "Bumbumbumbumbum." Her head dropped and her hands began working busily, picking at a button on her blouse.

"This isn't one of her better days," Mr. Willet whispered to Min and Flora. He turned to his wife. "Did you have a good morning, honey? It's nice to be out in the sunshine, isn't it?"

The old hands worried the button.

"Mrs. Willet," said Flora timidly, "we came to teach a class. A sewing class. We're going to make cases for eyeglasses."

"Bumbumbumbumbumbumbumbum."

"Well," said Mr. Willet, "I suppose we might as well go on to the activities room, but I know Mary Lou enjoyed your visit."

Flora watched as Min leaned down to kiss Mrs. Willet's soft cheek. "Good-bye, Mary Lou. I'll come back soon," she said.

Flora leaned down, too, and put her hands over Mrs. Willet's busy ones. The hands grew still. "It was nice to see you," said Flora. "I'll come back soon, too."

"Bye," said Mrs. Willet.

And Mr. Willet beamed at his wife.

The activities room was large and sunny and full of supplies and works in progress.

"Wow!" exclaimed Flora. "This is the best art room ever! It's like the art room at school times ten."

Mr. Willet laughed. "As you can tell, all kinds of

classes are held here. There are classes in sculpture and pottery and painting and woodcarving. Oh, and quilting." He pointed to a corner of the room where a large half-finished quilt was stretched across a frame.

Flora saw cupboards spilling over with paintbrushes and paints and ink and clay and papers and beads and rags and cleaners and tools. Tables and chairs were placed haphazardly around the room.

"All right," said Mr. Willet. "Nine people signed up for the class. Let's move some of the tables together to make one big one. We'll put the supplies in the middle. Does that sound all right, Min?"

"Perfect," she replied.

Flora was emptying the carton, setting out fabric and a stack of instructions, when the first student entered the room. He was a tall man, very thin, and he introduced himself as Mr. Selden.

"He's ninety-two years old," Mr. Willet whispered to Min and Flora.

"And my hearing is as sharp as ever," he said, and everyone laughed.

The people who gathered for the class were nothing like what Flora had imagined. They were lively and funny and they told wonderful stories. One woman had been a doctor and had practiced all over the world. Another had been a violinist and had played with orchestras in Los Angeles and Chicago. "Once," she said, "I met Leonard Bernstein." Mr. Selden was a writer. "But I never wrote any books for children," he said to Flora. "Although I did write about a dog once. You might like that book." There were a husband and wife who told Flora about their recent trip to China. "We plan to go back next year," the woman added.

When the introductions were over, Min stood and faced the students. "Welcome to 'And Sew On and Sew Forth,' the first of three classes my granddaughter and I will be teaching," she said. "Before we begin, please tell me how many of you would say that you have more than beginning sewing skills." To Flora's surprise, all of the students, including Mr. Willet, raised their hands.

And later, after Flora had handed around the instructions and the pattern for the case that Min had drawn up, the students began the project immediately.

"I don't think we have anything to teach you!" exclaimed Min as nine pairs of hands busied themselves cutting and measuring, matching fabrics, and selecting embroidery floss.

"Oh, yes, you do," said the woman who had met Leonard Bernstein. "I only know how to do basic embroidery. I want you to teach me how to make a bullion knot."

"And I've never made anything like the silk flower

you mention here," said Mr. Selden, pointing to the instruction sheet. "I'll need help with that."

The two hours passed quickly. Flora flew from one student to another, giving advice, demonstrating sewing tricks, and occasionally calling on Min for help. At one point, Flora glanced into the hallway and saw Nikki's mother. "Hi, Mrs. Sherman!" she called.

Mrs. Sherman grinned. "Hello, Flora. I'm in a rush," she replied. "But it's nice to see you." She hurried on.

"You know Mrs. Sherman?" asked Mr. Selden. When Flora nodded, he said, "She's a wonderful addition to our community." Flora smiled, thinking how happy this bit of news would make Nikki.

At the end of the class, not one of the glasses cases had been completed, but they were mostly finished and everyone was eager to return to their apartments to get back to work.

"We'll see you on Wednesday," said Min as she and Flora gathered up the supplies. "Get ready to learn basic paper piecing."

"Are you going home now?" Flora asked Mr. Willet.

"No. Not yet. I'm going to spend some more time with Mary Lou." He glanced at Min and cleared his throat. "I guess there's no good time to tell you this," he went on. "I've decided to move to Three Oaks as soon as an apartment becomes available. I'm about to put my house on the market."

"Oh, Bill," said Min. "Really? I understand, of course, but, oh, we're going to miss you."

"And I'll miss you, all of you. And my home." He spread his hands before him. "I just don't know what else to do."

"Getting old isn't easy, is it?" asked Min.

"No. But, as my father used to say, it beats the alternative."

Min and Mr. Willet both smiled, but their smiles were so sad that Flora thought she might cry.

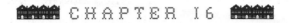 

# CHAPTER 16

# Olivia, Olivia

Every now and then, Olivia Walter liked to have a conversation with herself. She usually did this in bed, and on those evenings when she felt she needed a conversation, she said good night to her family unusually early. Then she would lie on her back in her pajamas, gaze into the gathering darkness, and imagine two Olivias, dressed identically, as if she had a twin. Also, she would imagine that they were the only two people in the world. Just Olivia and Olivia. And nothing mattered but their conversation.

On a Wednesday night in mid-August, Olivia decided it was time for a conversation. So she said good night to her mother and her father, to Henry and Jack, and retired to her room. She peeked in the hamster cage and said good night to Sandy. Then she climbed into bed and turned out her light. She squinted at the ceiling, and soon the two Olivias were before her.

"Look," said one Olivia. "It's just after eight-thirty, and the only light in here is from street lamps. A month ago, there would still have been the last little bit of daylight now. The days are getting shorter."

"Don't remind me," replied the second Olivia. "A month from *now*, we'll be back in school."

"The big school."

"With Tanya."

"I'll bet Tanya never goes to bed early in order to have a conversation with herself."

"Maybe Tanya isn't a very creative person."

"Maybe Tanya is a very mature person."

"I could be mature."

"Do you want to be?"

"Not yet."

"Can you believe that everyone has replied to the party invitations *except* Tanya?"

"What do you think that means?"

"I hope it means that the Rhodeses are away and Tanya hasn't gotten the invitation yet."

"It probably does. Mom and Dad said August is the biggest vacation month of the summer."

"Everyone else is coming to the party."

"Wouldn't it be . . . what's the word? Ironic? Wouldn't it be ironic if Tanya was the only one who couldn't come to the party? Tanya was the whole *reason* for the party."

"Maybe Tanya is just rude and didn't bother to RSVP."

"I thought of that."

"I have another worry: What if the other guests are playing a trick? Maybe they said they were going to come, but they don't really intend to. What a joke it would be if I planned this big party and the only guests were Nikki, Ruby, and Flora."

"Try to think about something more pleasant."

"Hmm. The vegetable garden."

"Yes! The vegetable garden. Mr. Pennington said the four of us should be very proud of ourselves."

"I'm proud of us."

"Me, too. I didn't really think we'd be able to make a donation to the food bank with our own vegetables. But we did."

"Tomatoes and green peppers. The people at the food bank looked pretty happy to see us."

"Mr. Pennington said that in the fall we'll have a bumper crop of squash."

"I've never been sure what a bumper crop is, exactly."

"Remember to look it up tomorrow."

"Here's another happy thing: Nelson Day."

"Ruby's big idea. It *is* exciting. There's going to be a street fair on Main Street again, like last spring."

"The proceeds from the sidewalk sale will be donated to the Nelsons."

"There are going to be food vendors, too."

"And balloon rides, but I think they're going to be too expensive."

"I'm dying to ride in a hot air balloon. It must be so peaceful, floating around, looking down on everything. I'd be able to see Main Street from way up high."

Despite the conversation, and despite the fact that Olivia wanted to talk about the interesting turn the book club had taken, her eyes began to close. One of the two Olivias on the ceiling disappeared, and the one who was left fell silent. In Olivia's mind an enormous pink-and-green balloon descended slowly from the skies above Camden Falls, coming to a gentle landing in front of Sincerely Yours. A door in the basket of the balloon opened by itself, and Olivia stepped inside. She was all alone, rising and rising, watching Main Street fall away below her.

When Olivia awoke the next morning, the first thing she thought of was the balloon. She felt quite peaceful, and she told herself that in the future when she began to feel anxious about something she should call to mind the pink-and-green balloon and imagine a nice quiet ride somewhere.

Olivia had been up for less than five minutes that

morning when the phone rang and Jack shouted, "Olivia, it's for you!"

"Coming!" Olivia replied, and was horrified to hear Jack say conspiratorially to Henry, "Make that farting noise into the phone. Flora will think it's Olivia."

"Henry, don't you dare!" cried Olivia. "Jack, give me the phone! . . . Flora?"

"Hi! Did you remember what today is?"

"How could I forget?"

"Are you going to walk into town with Ruby and Min and me?"

"Sure. What time did Nikki say she'd be there?"

"Ten."

"Okay. I'll be over as soon as I can. I can't believe we have to wait until ten to open the letters, though."

Olivia flew back to her room, dressed in a hurry (in new clothes bought on a shopping spree with her mother the week before), and scanned her room for *Understood Betsy*, which had turned out to be the final book club selection. Three days earlier, Min Read had arrived at Needle and Thread and found a stack of envelopes by the door. Monday was not the usual day for the arrival of the envelopes, so when Flora phoned Olivia to say that the books had arrived, Olivia's heart quickened.

"Something's up," she'd said to Flora. "I can feel it. This isn't usual."

Sure enough, when the girls gathered at Needle and

Thread later and opened the envelopes, they found that the letter accompanying *Understood Betsy* said only, "First read the book. Your final letter will arrive in three days."

That was it. Nothing more.

"No list of things to talk about," said Flora.

"No Saturday activity," said Nikki.

Ruby had squinted her eyes and said in a thickly accented voice, "Veddy, veddy strange." When she realized that the other girls were staring at her, she added, "I'm a foreign detective."

Olivia had spent the next three days reading *Understood Betsy*, by Dorothy Canfield. At first she had found the story of Elizabeth Ann, orphaned as a baby, who at age nine moves to the Vermont countryside to live with her aunt and uncle, to be old-fashioned (the story took place in the early 1900s) and a bit babyish. But the more she read, the better she liked the story. Betsy, as her relatives call her, might be only nine years old, but the things she does on her own — well, Olivia certainly couldn't imagine doing them herself. They might have seemed small on the surface, but if you thought about them, they were really rather momentous. Walking to a new school all by yourself without even knowing where the school is! Getting lost at a fair and having to find your way home at a time when there were no telephones or cars.

Bravery, thought Olivia. Once again, one of the themes of the book club selection was bravery.

Olivia had read the book with relish, all the time wondering what the final letter would say.

And now it was Thursday, and she would soon find out.

Olivia, Flora, Ruby, and Min turned the corner onto Main Street — and Olivia broke into a run. "Come on!" she called, and Flora and Ruby hurried after her.

The envelopes that lay in the corner of the doorway to Needle and Thread were small.

"Just regular envelopes," observed Ruby.

"I think *Understood Betsy* was our last book," said Olivia sadly.

The girls sat on the couches at the front of the store and stared at the letters. Olivia willed Nikki to hurry. "Come earlier, come earlier, come earlier," she chanted silently.

But it was after ten when Nikki ran through the door.

"Here! Here!" exclaimed Ruby, thrusting an envelope into Nikki's hand. "We can't wait a single second longer. One, two, three, open!"

In a flash, the four letters were opened. Flora let out a gasp.

"What is it, girls?" called Min from the checkout counter.

There was a tangle of voices as the four girls tried to answer at the same time.

"How about if one of you reads the letter aloud to me?" suggested Min.

"I'll do it! I'll do it!" said Olivia. "Well, first there are the things to think about and discuss and stuff. But the last paragraph says, 'Your fourth and final adventure will take place this Saturday. Please gather at Flora and Ruby's house at seven-thirty in the morning.'"

"That's a little early, isn't it?" said Ruby, and Min muttered something about sloths.

Olivia ignored the question. "'At seven-thirty in the morning,'" she resumed, "'for a trip to Sands Point. Be prepared to spend the day there. The person who will be taking you on the trip is the creator of the book club.' *And*," said Olivia with relish, "the —"

"The letter is signed Madame X!" cried Ruby triumphantly.

Olivia glared at Ruby, but Ruby seemed not to notice.

"Madame X," repeated Nikki, eyes narrowed. "So. The mystery person is a woman."

"I kind of thought it might be Mr. Pennington," said Olivia.

"I wondered if it might be Sonny. He works in the bookstore and everything," said Flora.

"I hate to ask this, but what's Sands Point?" asked Nikki.

"Yeah, what is it?" asked Flora and Ruby at the same time.

"Am I the only one who knows Sands Point?" said Olivia. "Well, you guys are going to love it. It's a town from the early nineteen hundreds. You walk into it and feel like you've stepped back in time."

"Oh, into Betsy's time!" Nikki said. "I get it. We're going to visit the time in which the story took place. Cool."

"But even more cool, we'll finally find out who the mystery person is," said Ruby.

"Let's have our book talk now," said Flora.

Olivia and her friends tried hard, very hard, to concentrate on the list of things to talk about, but every few sentences, one of them would cry out, "I'll bet Madame X is Gigi!" or "Maybe Mary Woolsey is Madame X!"

Finally, Ruby pointed to Olivia and said, "Maybe *you're* Madame X!"

Olivia laughed. But then she thought, Madame X could be Nikki or Flora. Or Ruby — the one who dared to suggest that the mystery person was one of us. She eyed her friends suspiciously. And then she said, "Forty-eight hours from now, we'll know who Madame X *really* is."

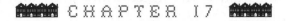

# CHAPTER 17

# *Madame X*

Nikki was in such a state of excitement about Madame X's identity and the trip to Sands Point that she asked if she could spend Friday night at Olivia's house. Olivia then asked if she and Nikki could spend Friday night with Flora and Ruby, so a slumber party was arranged.

"But," said Min, "I strongly suggest that you have an actual slumber party — in other words, that you *sleep* on Friday night. You won't have much fun at Sands Point if you've been up all the night before."

And the girls did sleep. Except for ten minutes shortly after three o'clock, when Ruby got up to go to the bathroom, returned to her sister's room, and woke Nikki, Olivia, and Flora to say, "What if Madame X is Mrs. Grindle!"

By seven-fifteen the next morning, Nikki and her friends were sitting in a row on Min's front stoop. At Min's insistence, each was wearing a hat and had slathered herself with sunscreen since they were going to be outdoors all day.

"I feel like I'm waiting to go on a field trip," said Nikki.

"A field trip conducted by a mysterious stranger," said Flora.

"You know, once on *I Love Lucy*," said Ruby, "there was a person named Madame X and she was a *burglar!*"

"Min wouldn't let us go off with a burglar," said Flora.

"Oh, what *time* is it?" huffed Olivia, peering at her watch.

"Twenty seconds since the last time someone asked what time it is," said Nikki.

Flora stood and looked up and down Aiken Avenue. "There are hardly any cars out at all."

After a short silence, Olivia announced, "It's seven-twenty-nine."

"There's a car!" cried Ruby. But it drove past the Row Houses.

"There's a van!" said Nikki. "And it's slowing down!"

The girls stared. The van pulled to a stop in front of Min's house.

"Oh, it's only Aunt Allie," said Flora in a low voice. "What's she doing here?"

"Maybe she's coming along to Sands Point," whispered Olivia. "You know, like a volunteer on a field trip."

Aunt Allie waved to the girls. She was grinning.

"Oh, no," said Ruby suddenly as she watched her aunt climb out of the van. "Oh, *no*. You guys, Aunt Allie is" (Ruby lowered her voice to a whisper) "Madame X."

Nikki stared at Ruby. Everyone else was staring at Aunt Allie.

At that moment, Min's front door opened. Flora turned around. "Min? Is it true? Aunt Allie is Madame X?"

"True as true," replied Min. "Everybody ready? I'm going to come with you."

"Ha!" cried Ruby. "I knew you were coming! I saw you putting on sunscreen, too."

Aunt Allie stood on the lawn facing the girls. For a moment, no one spoke, and Nikki saw disappointment cross Allie's face.

Nikki smiled at her. "Madame X," she said. "Thank you for the book club. We had a wonderful summer."

Aunt Allie's grin returned. "Did you? Did you really?"

"Oh, it was the best surprise!" exclaimed Flora, recovering.

"We loved the books you chose," added Olivia.

"I read all of them," said Ruby.

With that, everyone began to talk at once.

"You knew about the secret from the very beginning, didn't you, Min?" said Flora, and Min smiled.

"It was so hard to keep the secret!" exclaimed Aunt Allie. "You almost caught me buying copies of *The Summer of the Swans*, Nikki. Sonny was helping me in Time and Again, and in you walked. I had to hide in the store until you left! You almost caught me once, too, Ruby."

"When did you deliver the envelopes?" Ruby wanted to know.

"What did you do on Brave Saturday?" asked Aunt Allie.

Min held her hands up. "Wait!" she said. "Let's get in the van and talk on the way to Sands Point. We have a little trip ahead of us."

"Hey, that's another question," said Ruby. "Where did this van come from?"

"I borrowed it from a friend," Aunt Allie replied. "Okay, climb on in, everyone."

The drive to Sands Point was nearly an hour and a half long, but there was not a moment of silence as the van whizzed along past pine forests and clear, shining lakes and little spits of land ending in docks or fishermen's cabins.

"We had our best discussion of all about *Roll of*

*Thunder*," said Flora. "It made us think about *The Diary of Anne Frank*."

"My favorite book was *Mrs. Frisby*," said Ruby, "and I almost didn't finish it! I've never read five books in one summer."

"We liked having Saturday adventures," said Nikki. "That was a cool idea."

"What *did* you do on Brave Saturday?" asked Aunt Allie again.

"I can't say. Mine's private," Nikki replied uncomfortably.

"Oh. That's okay." Aunt Allie glanced in the rearview mirror at the girls. "You don't have to tell me what you did. I just thought —"

"I held a snake!" cried Flora.

Everyone laughed.

"She's been saying that at least once a day since she did it," said Olivia.

"Where did you find a snake?" asked Aunt Allie.

Flora told her how Brave Saturday had started off.

"Now you tell us something," Ruby said to her aunt. "When did you deliver the packages to the store?"

"In the evening. Not long after the store had closed. I figured they would be okay in the doorway overnight."

"Sneaky," said Ruby.

"We tried to catch you one morning," Olivia confessed.

"You mean, I did," said Nikki. "I played private detective. But you had already delivered the packages."

Min, who was sitting in the front with Allie, consulted the map that was spread across her knees. "We're going to turn onto Route Two Fourteen up here," she said. "We stay on that for about ten miles, and then we should start seeing signs for Sands Point."

"Hey," said Olivia, leaning forward in her seat and addressing Aunt Allie, "did you know that I'm the only one of us who's been to Sands Point before?"

"Min told me that Flora and Ruby hadn't been there," Allie replied, "but Nikki, I'm surprised you've never been. You grew up in Camden Falls, didn't you?"

"Yes," said Nikki. Outside her window the mountains had softened into low hills, and the earth was becoming sandier. "My family, well, we never really got to take trips or anything." The van rolled by a covered bridge. "But things are going to be different now, I think," she added. "Anyway, this is nice. Thank you very much for today."

Several miles later, Ruby suddenly cried, "Look! There's a big sign for Sands Point! We're almost there!"

Ten minutes later, Aunt Allie pulled into a parking lot, and soon Nikki and her friends were piling out of the van. "This is so exciting!" said Nikki. "Look at everyone."

The parking lot was a sea of cars and vans baking

in the August sun. Groups of people, chattering and laughing, walked toward the Sands Point entrance, and soon Min, Allie, and the members of the secret book club joined them.

"I feel like we're going to a fair," said Ruby.

Aunt Allie grinned. "That's how I used to feel when Min and Dad would bring your mother and me here."

"You and Mom used to come to Sands Point?" asked Flora in astonishment.

"Almost every summer. Oh, you should have seen our faces when Min would say it was time to go to Sands Point again."

"You should have heard their voices!" exclaimed Min. "Such shouting. But it was all part of the fun."

At the edge of the parking lot was a sign reading THIS WAY TO TOWN and an arrow pointing to a dirt lane.

"Follow me, ladies," said Aunt Allie.

Nikki, craning her neck to see ahead, followed Allie down the dirt lane. It ended in the center of a small village.

"Oh," said Nikki softly, "a town. A whole town. I know you said Sands Point was a town, Olivia, but somehow I thought it would be a little fake town, like you'd find at an amusement park or something. This is *real*. Well, almost real. Stores, houses, an old-fashioned bank . . ."

"Look, there's a horse and buggy!" cried Flora.

"There's someone churning butter," said Olivia, pointing to a woman working busily on the front porch of a small house.

"There's the Sweet Shoppie!" exclaimed Ruby.

"It's just pronounced 'shop,'" Flora told her. "The Sweet Shoppe."

"Whatever. Can we buy candy there?"

"Absolutely," said Aunt Allie. "But let's look around before we go shopping."

They spent the rest of the morning walking from building to building until Nikki felt as if she actually did live at the turn of the twentieth century. They visited a blacksmith shop, they watched a woman weaving on a loom, and they looked around a one-room schoolhouse.

"Just like the one Betsy goes to in Vermont," said Flora.

They entered a house at the edge of the town, and Olivia said, "This is the way I picture Uncle Henry and Aunt Abigail's house."

The sun was directly over their heads ("Isn't everyone thankful for the sunscreen?" asked Min) when Ruby declared that she was absolutely famished.

"Let's get lunch, then," said Aunt Allie. "There are several restaurants here."

"Do they have regular food in them?" asked Ruby. "Or the kind Betsy had to eat?" She recalled that Betsy's first meal at the farm had consisted of baked beans, creamed potatoes, cold ham, hot cocoa, and pancakes, and she didn't particularly want any of those things for lunch on this hot day.

"Regular food," replied Min, and Ruby let out a sigh of relief.

"Not to mention," added Aunt Allie, "that there's a bakery and the Sweet Shoppe, as well as penny candy in the general store. You'll have plenty of things to choose from for dessert."

After lunch and dessert, the girls begged to go off on their own. *"Please?"* said Flora. "We'll be safe here. And we'll stay in pairs."

So Aunt Allie and Min set off in one direction, Ruby and Olivia in another, and Nikki and Flora in yet another.

"This is SO cool," Nikki said to Flora. "Really. It's better than any school field trip. And it was so nice of your aunt."

"I know," said Flora, frowning a little. "Who'd have thought . . . I mean . . . Aunt Allie . . . and she's not forcing us to eat, you know, spinach and bulgur wheat or something. She even bought candy herself. She's been fun today."

"I think she's trying really hard," said Nikki. "And I think that's what the book club has been all about. She wanted to do something special for you and Ruby, something you and she could talk about that would bring the three of you together."

Flora nodded. "It's a little hard to know what to say."

"Aren't you happy?" asked Nikki.

"Oh, I am. But . . . Ruby and I haven't been very nice about Aunt Allie."

"She isn't an easy person to like — which isn't your fault, Flora. Don't feel bad. Maybe this is your aunt's way of saying, 'Let's start over.'"

"Maybe."

"Come on, don't spoil it. She's offering you a way to make things better."

"That's true. Hey, I have an idea. Let's go back to the general store."

In the store, Flora, who had exactly seven dollars and forty-two cents, walked up and down and up and down the aisles, scrutinizing small items, touching them, comparing. At last she selected a small wooden plaque in the shape of a house, the words HOME SWEET HOME carved into a banner that looped across the roof, and she paid the cashier for it.

Later, as Min, Allie, and four weary girls were settling into the van to start the trip home, Flora handed the plaque to her aunt. "This is for you," she said. "For your new house. Thank you for today."

Aunt Allie held Flora in her gaze. "You're welcome," she replied, and turned around to clasp Flora's hand.

The passengers in the van were quiet on the ride back to Camden Falls, and Nikki was starting to doze, her head lolling against the window, when Ruby said wistfully, "I'm going to miss our Saturday adventures."

Nikki opened her eyes and murmured, "Who says they have to end? Let's have them all fall."

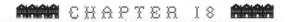 

# CHAPTER 18

# *Lost and Found*

"Town is busy today," Mrs. Edwards said to Robby as they walked along Main Street one morning.

"Mr. Walter said if the weather holds up, the last week in August will be very busy," Robby replied. "That is exactly what he said. 'If the weather holds up.'" He paused. "Does that mean if we have nice weather?"

"It does," said his mother. "And I guess he was right, since today is lovely —"

"And all the stores look busy," said Robby as they passed Needle and Thread.

"Ready for work?"

"Yes," Robby replied seriously. He had not forgotten about his bad day. The memory had faded, but it wasn't gone. And every time he remembered the glass ornament — the very expensive glass ornament — he noticed an uncomfortable sensation in his stomach.

"Okay, then. I'll see you this afternoon." Mrs. Edwards took her son's hand and leaned forward to kiss him on the cheek.

"Mom!" Robby cried, and pulled away from her. "Please! Not here. I'm a professional now." He shook his mother's hand and entered Sincerely Yours.

The store was already crowded. Robby checked the coffeepot, which was empty, put his things away, and called, "Hi, Mrs. Walter! Hi, Mr. Walter! I'll make the coffee now!"

His voice was loud, and several customers turned to look at him, but Robby concentrated on his job. When the coffee was brewing, he walked up and down the aisles, straightening the merchandise. "We're all out of lavender soap!" he yelled to Mr. Walter.

Robby reached the aisle containing the more fragile items. He glanced at the picture frames and decided not to straighten them. Then he glanced at the ornaments, felt the pang in his stomach, and gave them a wide berth. He wondered how long the sight of the ornaments would make him feel this way. Would that one bad day remain with him forever?

The morning passed quickly. The door to Sincerely Yours opened and closed, opened and closed. Customers asked for help. Mrs. Walter brought tray after tray of chocolates to the counter at the front of the store. Robby answered questions and helped at the cash register and avoided the glass ornaments.

At lunchtime, the store grew quiet briefly, and Mr. Walter sat down and said, "Oh, my aching feet."

The lull didn't last long. By one-thirty, the store was crowded again. Robby was helping a woman (a friend of Min's, he thought) select items to put in a birthday basket when he heard a shout.

No, not a shout, he realized. A scream. An actual scream like on television programs.

Startled, Robby turned around. Maybe someone had broken something. His eyes strayed to the picture frames, but no shards of glass glittered on the floor.

A second scream made Robby put his hands to his ears. He saw that the awful sound was coming from a young woman standing by the cash register. "My baby is gone!" she cried.

In seconds, a crowd had gathered around her.

"Try to calm down," said Mrs. Walter, emerging from the back of the store. "Tell us what happened. Your baby is gone?"

"My — my little girl," the woman replied. "Kirsten. She's four years old. She was right next to me and then I turned around and she was gone. She's nowhere in sight. I've looked everywhere! Oh, where *is* she?"

"I'm sure she's still here somewhere," said Mr. Walter calmly. "There are lots of good hiding places in the store. What does Kirsten look like?"

"She has brown hair and brown eyes and she's wearing red shorts and a white T-shirt. It says Camp

Seewackamano on the back of the shirt." The woman began to cry again.

"Come with me," said Mrs. Walter, taking her hand. "Let's search the back of the store. Maybe Kirsten wanted to see what was in the kitchen."

"Robby, help me look out here in front," said Mr. Walter.

"Roger," said Robby. He got down on his hands and knees and peered under things and behind things, and then he remembered the stockroom and searched it thoroughly.

"I don't see her," he said a few minutes later.

"She's not in the back," said Mrs. Walter.

Mr. Walter and Mrs. Walter and Robby and the crying woman, whose name turned out to be Marcia Perrone, all looked at one another. They were surrounded by silent customers, who were also looking at them.

"I think it's time to call the police," said Mr. Walter grimly, and he reached for the phone.

"Oh, no!" said Mrs. Perrone, and she let out a sob, which Robby thought was strange because aren't the police supposed to help?

Suddenly it seemed to Robby that everyone in the store was talking at once, and very loudly.

"I'll look outside."

"I'll go with you."

"I hope she has a picture of Kirsten with her. She'll need to give it to the police."

"Where's the police station? How long will it take them to get here?"

Robby put his hands over his ears again. This was terrible. Everything was too, too loud. He paused. Maybe all the noise was why Kirsten had left Sincerely Yours. Maybe she didn't like noise and confusion and crowded stores.

Robby glanced at the Walters, who were hovering around Mrs. Perrone, telling her to sit down and offering her a glass of water. Then he slipped out the door and stood on the sidewalk. He drew in a deep breath, let it out, drew in another. He looked up and down Main Street and thought how much he liked the sight of the trees, leafy and elegant, and the little stores with their cheerful windows. Bud's hot dog cart was parked in front of the Gourmet Shop, and Robby noticed a new blue-and-white-striped umbrella over the cart.

The sight of Main Street, sparkling in the sun, made Robby think of Main Street USA at Disney World. And *that* made him remember the time he got lost when he and his parents were on vacation there.

Robby closed his eyes. Lost. He had gotten lost at Disney World. Just like Kirsten was lost now. What had he done then? He cast his mind back eight years. Robby could feel the panic now that he had felt as a ten-year-old when he had turned around in a store and realized he didn't see either of his parents. He saw lots of other parents and lots of other kids and rows of T-shirts and pens and princess dresses and mouse ears and candy and sunglasses. And then he was aware of the noise. Kids were shouting and kids were crying and a dad was laughing and the cash registers were pinging and someone was talking *so* loudly on a cell phone and then someone dropped something with a *CRASH* and suddenly all Robby had wanted was to get away from the noise, noise, noise. So he had put his hands over his ears and run to another store that was much quieter, and soon his parents found him.

Robby opened his eyes. If he were Kirsten, he would look for a place that was peaceful. What was nearby that was peaceful? Across the street was Time and Again, the bookstore. That was always peaceful. But Robby had a feeling that Kirsten hadn't tried to cross the street. He looked to his left and looked to his right and saw that fewer people were to his right. So he walked in that direction, past the grocery store, and found that he was standing in front of the Fongs' studio and gallery.

Ah-ha, thought Robby. This was probably the most peaceful place on all of Main Street. The gallery on the ground floor was large, with high ceilings and sculptures on pedestals and nice paintings on the walls (some of them were pictures of just colors, not objects, and Robby liked those quite a bit), and soft, soothing music was always playing. Robby had not figured out where it came from; it seemed to float in the air.

Robby opened the door, stepped into the gallery, saw Mr. Fong talking with a customer in the back — and in the middle of the room next to a sculpture of a horse stood a small brown-haired girl wearing red shorts and a white T-shirt. Robby hurried to her, and then just to be *sure* she was Kirsten, he stepped around behind her and saw that written in an arc across the back of her shirt were the words CAMP SEEWACKAMANO.

Robby stepped around to her front again and said, "Are you lost?" The girl nodded and Robby realized she'd been crying. "Is your name Kirsten?" he asked.

Kirsten nodded.

"I know where your mother is," said Robby. "I can take you to her." He held out his hand.

But Kirsten shook her head. "I'm not allowed to go with strangers," she replied.

Robby knew that rule, all right, but it wasn't very helpful just now. Still, a rule was a rule. "Okay," said Robby. Then he hurried to Mr. Fong and said in a rush, "Mr. Fong, that little girl" (he pointed to Kirsten) "is lost and her mother is at Sincerely Yours and the police are coming and she won't go with a stranger, so I'm going to bring her mother back here."

Mr. Fong frowned. "What?" he said, but Robby was already running out the door. He sprinted to Sincerely Yours, shouted, "Mrs. Perrone, I found your baby but she won't go with a stranger so I left her with Mr. Fong. Just follow me and you can get her back!"

Mrs. Perrone wasn't the only one who followed Robby to the gallery. A crowd of people came rushing along after them — Mrs. Walter and quite a few customers and a police officer and Robby wasn't sure who else. When Mrs. Perrone saw Kirsten, she grabbed her and hugged her and cried and laughed and scolded her all at the same time.

Mrs. Walter turned to Robby then and said, "You're a hero!" and someone snapped his picture and later it appeared in the newspaper and Robby decided this had been the best day of his whole life.

# CHAPTER 19

# Brave Saturday, Part Two

Parties, Olivia thought, were so much more fun and easier to plan when you were little. A birthday party, for instance, involved musical chairs, pin the tail on the donkey, a scavenger hunt, goody bags all around, a pile of presents to open, and pizza and cake and ice cream. Period, the end. Olivia still thought this was the best kind of party and wished, in fact, that the party she was giving — this very afternoon — could be just that (even though it wasn't her birthday).

But, thought Olivia with a sigh, she was going into seventh grade and parties were different now. Of course, she might have a better idea of just what went on at a seventh-grade party if she had been invited to Tanya's. But she hadn't. She'd been crossed off the list (or so she assumed).

And yet, here she was, getting ready to give a party

to which she'd invited not only Tanya (the list-crosser-offer) but everyone else who'd been at Tanya's party. Olivia thought over the events of the summer — the humiliation of not receiving an invitation even though Nikki and Flora had been invited (and everyone *knew* that the three of them were best friends), her plans for Brave Saturday, dropping her invitations in the mailbox so that there was no going back, and then waiting to see if anyone (other than Nikki, Ruby, and Flora) would RSVP. And now it was the last Saturday of August, which was also the last Saturday of summer vacation — school would start in three days — and Olivia's party was to take place in the afternoon.

She still had not heard from Tanya.

Everyone else was coming, but Tanya was a question mark.

Olivia sat on her bed that morning and looked out onto the familiar sight of Aiken Avenue, a view she had seen nearly every day of her life. There was Mr. Pennington's tidy front yard, there was the rosebush in Min's yard, there was the oak tree, the lamppost, the fire hydrant. Olivia wished she could spend the rest of summer vacation sitting in her safe, familiar room. She didn't want to give a party, not this party, anyway. But everything had been set in motion.

Olivia reached for the phone and dialed Flora.

"Hi!" said Flora. "Are you excited about today?"

"No."

"Really? You're not? You're just nervous?"

"Yeah. And I want it to be over with. But I also want it to go well."

"It will. It'll go well."

"How do you know? This isn't the kind of party Tanya would give. And why didn't Tanya ever reply to the invitation, anyway?"

Flora sighed. "Olivia, I don't know."

"Everyone else replied. And now Melody and all those friends of Tanya's, the ones who tease me and are jealous of my grades, are going to be there. Oh, *why* did I decide to have a party?"

"Because of Brave Saturday," Flora replied. "This is a very brave thing you're doing, Olivia. Just like all the brave characters we read about this summer."

"I guess. But that doesn't mean the party is going to go well. It could be a big, giant disaster, and I —"

"Olivia, back up. Why *did* you want to give the party in the first place?"

"To — I guess to kind of remind the other girls that I'm — that I'm *here*. And I'm a nice person. And to point out that maybe we could all be friends."

"Okay. Well, I think the party is going to do every one of those things. Besides, you came up with a great idea: Who else do you know who could have a party in her family's own store?"

"You," said Olivia.

"Okay, that's true. But a party at Sincerely Yours is going to be so cool."

"Are you sure? It's not the same as a pool party and barbecue. And *I* like my idea, but that doesn't mean anyone else will."

"Are you kidding? The guests get to put together their own gift baskets. Your mom and dad said they can take anything they want from the store."

"Within reason. I think there's going to be a limit. They can't choose something that costs a hundred dollars. But most of the stuff's not expensive anyway."

"See? That's great! They'll love it. It'll be just like the time Maura had her birthday party in that place where you make your own pottery."

"I guess."

"Olivia! Quit worrying, or the party really won't go well. Now, come on. What time are Ruby and I supposed to be at the store?"

"Mom and Dad are going to close it at four this afternoon. You guys and Nikki come at four-thirty, okay? Everyone else is coming at five."

"I'll see you at four-thirty."

"Well?" Olivia said to her friends as they looked around Sincerely Yours that afternoon. "What do you think?"

"It's . . . it's beautiful!" exclaimed Nikki. "Really wonderful. It's all glittery."

Olivia and her father had strung tiny white lights on the shelves and the candy counter and around the door and the window. In the front of the store a table had been set out and on it were trays of chocolates and brownies and cookies made by Mrs. Walter.

"We'll order pizzas later," said Olivia. "So . . . first we'll just talk and stuff and have snacks, then everyone can make the gift baskets, and after that we'll get pizzas. Is that enough for a party? I mean, enough to do? I know it isn't like Tanya's —"

"Olivia," said Nikki, "it's plenty, really." She gave her friend a hug.

"Do you have stage fright, Olivia?" asked Ruby.

"I guess. A little. What do you do when you have stage fright?"

"Yoga."

"Oh. I guess there isn't time for that."

"Nope," said Ruby, "because the first person is here."

Olivia let out a shriek and looked toward the door.

"It's Melody," said Nikki in a low voice.

"And Tanya's with her!" exclaimed Olivia. "So. She's just a rude person who doesn't RSVP."

"Olivia — get over it," whispered Flora.

Olivia, an awful, heavy feeling in her stomach, opened the door to Sincerely Yours. "Hi," she said. "Come on in."

Melody and Tanya, arm in arm, entered the store.

"Hi, Flora! Hi, Nikki!" they chorused as they stepped around Olivia.

Olivia felt like a dead fish on a beach, pairs of bare feet carefully avoiding her.

Her mother stepped forward. "Girls, I'm Mrs. Walter, and this is Mr. Walter. And surely you know Olivia," she added pointedly.

Olivia was pleased to see Tanya flush slightly. "Hi," said Tanya.

"Um, well," Olivia began, "help yourselves." She indicated the trays of treats. "My mom made all these things."

"Cool," said Melody.

The door opened again and in came Claudette Tisch and Mary Louise Detwiler. "Hi, Olivia! Thank you for inviting us!"

The heaviness in Olivia's stomach began to lighten. Sophie Pearson arrived, and then two girls from Mrs. Annich's class. And before Olivia knew it, Sincerely Yours was filled with kids who were laughing and talking and calling to one another. And Olivia was among them. Claudette asked Olivia what she had done over the summer, and Olivia told her about the secret book club.

"Wow," said Claudette. "You are so lucky."

Melody pulled Olivia aside and said, "This is your family's store?"

"Yup."

"I've been in here before, but I didn't know it was yours."

"We're all going to make our own gift baskets in a few minutes," Olivia told her proudly, and was gratified to see Melody's eyes widen.

"Really?" said Melody.

"Yup."

It suddenly occurred to Olivia that someone was going to have to make an announcement about this. "Um, Ruby," she said, "do you want to stand on a chair and tell everyone that they can start putting their baskets together?"

"Sure!" said Ruby.

But Nikki pulled Olivia aside and said, "You have to do it, Olivia. Not Ruby."

Olivia compromised. She lifted a stack of baskets down from one of the shelves, passed them around, and told her guests — individually — that they could start taking things from the shelves. "You could put together a basket for yourself, or for one of your friends, or your mom or dad. Or you could make a special-occasion basket, like for a birthday." She glanced at her father.

"The only rule," added Mr. Walter, "is that the value of the basket can't be more than twenty-five dollars."

"Cool!" said Sophie. "Olivia, this is the best party."

"Really?" replied Olivia. "Thank you."

Flora, standing nearby with Ruby, saw the relief and pleasure on her friend's face. She also saw the grim set of Tanya's jaw and was about to say something to Nikki when Ruby tugged on her shirt. Flora leaned over and Ruby whispered in her ear, "That girl" (she tried to indicate Tanya without pointing at her) "is jealous. Who is she?"

"Tanya. That's Tanya."

"The one who didn't invite Olivia to her party."

Flora nodded.

"I don't like her," said Ruby.

"Give her a chance. She was nice to Nikki and me."

Olivia, having handed the baskets around, now found herself in the middle of a group of girls.

"Do you work here? I mean, do you get to help out at the store?" asked Claudette.

"Sure," said Olivia. "Anytime I want."

"And your mom makes all the candy and stuff?"

Olivia nodded. "She has help, but these are her own recipes. And she comes up with the ideas for things like the chocolate numbers to put on birthday cakes, and chocolate candles. You can't light them, but you can eat them."

The girls laughed.

"Does your mom make candy at home, too?" asked Mary Louise.

"She used to, but now she mostly makes it here. To sell."

Tanya joined the girls. "Hey, Olivia. What did you do this summer? Did you go away?"

Olivia shook her head. "Flora and Nikki and Ruby and I were really busy, though. And also, I worked on my butterfly collection. I only collect dead butterflies, though. I never kill live ones. I have butterflies from . . ." Olivia's voice trailed off. She saw Tanya nudge Melody. "Well, anyway, I was busy."

"Look, you guys," said Claudette, who was standing before a display of rattles and rubber duckies. "I put together a basket of baby things. I'm going to become an aunt this fall, you know. My big sister is having a baby."

"My basket," said Nikki, who had been studying the candy counter, "is for my brother. Tomorrow he leaves for college."

Tanya turned her attention from Olivia to Nikki. "Your brother is going to college?"

Nikki nodded. "He got in over the summer. And he got a scholarship."

"Wow. I thought . . ."

Nikki glared at Tanya.

"Um, well, my basket is going to be for my mother," said Tanya quickly.

"Come on, then," said Melody. "I'll show you where the candles are. You should put a candle in her basket."

The girls fell silent, and finally Olivia said, "So what did you guys do over the summer?"

"I was a CIT at this camp in Maine," said Sophie. "For a month. It was so cool. Every Saturday night the CITs at the girls' camp got to go to the boys' camp and have a picnic or something with the boy CITs."

"I helped out with the summer program for the kids at the community pool," said Mary Louise. "Lots of cute lifeguards there."

Claudette and Sophie and Mary Louise laughed.

Olivia took a step back, nearly stumbling into Tanya.

"Pizza time!" announced her mother. "Are you girls almost done with your baskets?"

"Yes!" everyone chorused.

"How did you do?"

Claudette held out her baby basket, and Nikki held out her basket for Tobias, and soon the girls were exclaiming and talking and comparing items. Olivia felt Flora nudge her into the group again. She was relieved when the pizzas arrived.

An hour later, the pizzas devoured, Mr. Detwiler peeked through the window of Sincerely Yours. Claudette's parents were behind him, and the next thing Olivia knew, her guests were calling, "Goodbye!" and "Thank you!" and "See you in school!"

Her party was over.

● × ● × ●

Later, in bed, Olivia decided to have another conversation with herself.

"It went okay, don't you think?" asked one of the Olivias.

"The most important thing is that I did it. Tanya didn't invite me to her party, but I went ahead and had a party of my own and invited her to it."

"That was the adult thing to do."

"I think so."

"And everyone had a good time."

"Including me. It was fun talking to the other girls."

"What about the butterfly collection?"

"I can't think about that. I shouldn't have mentioned it. I'll have to be very careful about what I say once school starts."

The Olivias began to swim and float, and in her bed below, Olivia Walter's eyes drooped and she fell asleep to owl calls and Jacques barking and all the nighttime sounds of Aiken Avenue.

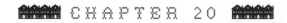 

# CHAPTER 20

# Good-bye, Tobias

Nikki tried not to eat too much pizza at Olivia's party. It was hard to turn down perfectly good free pizza, but she knew that when she got home, she and her mother and Mae were going to have a good-bye dinner for Tobias.

As Nikki bicycled along the lane leading to her house, she tried to imagine evenings — months and years of them stretching away before her — without Tobias close by. She had told her brother not to worry, that she and Mae and her mother would be fine. This was the twenty-first century, for lord's sake, and women didn't need men to take care of them. They could take care of themselves. But when Nikki thought, really thought, about long, dark hours with no Tobias in the next room, an uneasy feeling crept over her. She shook it off now as she rode along. Tobias was ready to leave — he deserved this opportunity — and she did not want to be responsible for his changing his mind.

"Hi, everyone! I'm home!" Nikki called.

"We're in the kitchen," her mother replied.

Nikki entered the kitchen to find the table set with the floral cloth they had used the previous Christmas and a vase of wildflowers (picked by Mae, she suspected) flanked by red candles.

"Mom, the table looks beautiful," said Nikki.

"Thanks, honey. How was the party?"

"It was great. Look what I made for Tobias." Nikki held out the basket she had carefully ridden home on her bicycle. "Everyone got to make one. Whatever kind they wanted."

"That was awfully nice of the Walters."

"They knew how important the party was to Olivia."

Mrs. Sherman removed a pot of spaghetti from the stove, set it down on a dish towel, and considered her daughter. "Would you like to have a party sometime, honey? You've never had one, not even a birthday party."

"That's okay, Mom. Really. I don't need a party."

"But we could afford one now."

And, thought Nikki, Dad isn't around anymore to frighten off the guests. "I know, but it's not important to me in the same way it was to Olivia. It's kind of hard to explain. Maybe Mae should have a birthday party, though, when she turns eight."

"Who's having a party?" Tobias, grinning, staggered down the stairs carrying two suitcases and a pillow.

"Nobody yet," replied Nikki.

"I am!" cried Mae. She ran through the front door, Paw-Paw at her heels. "I heard you guys through the window. You said I could have a party!"

"When you turn eight," said her mother.

"Goody. Tobias, look at the table. It's as fancy as Christmas. Remember when we set the table with the angels and the candles and the bowl of pinecones? 'Course, we don't have angels or pinecones now, but —"

"Mae," said Mrs. Sherman, "try to calm down a little, please."

"The table looks great," said Tobias. He set his things by the front door.

"I can't believe you're actually leaving tomorrow," said Nikki.

"Me, neither," replied Tobias. "But I am."

Upstairs in his room, Nikki knew, was a stack of papers and letters related to Tobias's freshman year at Leavitt College. Maps, too. All on his own, Tobias had made the arrangements for arriving at school, including getting directions for driving himself there. Nikki had seen plenty of television shows about students going off to college for the first time, and in all of them, the parents and their kid loaded up the family station wagon (packed so tightly that the driver couldn't see out the back window) and drove to the college together. Once there, the parents talked with other parents and met professors and maybe even the president of the college, saw their son or daughter safely settled into a dorm room (having introduced themselves to the roommates and *their* parents), and made sure their kid had a checking account set up with a nice sum of money in it, before finally saying good-bye.

But the next morning, Tobias would drive off to Leavitt College by himself. Mrs. Sherman needed to put in half a day at work, and in any case, she had no idea about colleges and professors and dorms and roommates. Tobias said he would be fine, and Nikki believed him. But she could not imagine being in his shoes and sincerely hoped that when the time came for her to leave for college, her mother would drive her there no matter what.

"Everybody ready for dinner?" asked Mrs. Sherman.

"Yes," chorused Nikki and Mae.

"I have a few more loads," said Tobias, "but I'll take them out to the car after dinner."

"How come you're taking them out now?" asked Mae. "You aren't leaving until tomorrow. Are you?" she added suspiciously.

"I want to get an early start in the morning."

"Tobias? I don't want you to —"

Nikki grabbed her sister by the elbow. "Get your plate, Mae. Mom made spaghetti."

Mae reached for her plate.

When the Shermans were seated around their kitchen table, Tobias said, "Wow. My last dinner here."

"But not your last dinner here forever," his mother pointed out. "You'll be back for holidays and vacations."

"And maybe in between," said Tobias. "Leavitt isn't all that far away. I can come home on weekends sometimes." He paused. "If you need me."

"We'll be just fine."

"We'll be great," said Nikki.

She had taken exactly one forkful of spaghetti (and was just thinking that perhaps it had been a teensy bit too big) when she heard the sound of tires on the Shermans' unpaved drive.

Mrs. Sherman, Tobias, Nikki, and Mae put down their forks and looked at one another.

"Are we expecting anyone?" asked Tobias.

"I don't think so," said his mother.

Nikki was struck with two thoughts then — two thoughts of great import — and also managed to marvel at how one's brain could generate more than one thought in the same second. Her first thought was: What if it's *Dad* who's driving up our lane right now?

Her second thought was: What would Mom and Mae and I do if Dad came back while Tobias was away?

Brain racing, stomach dropping, Nikki leaped to her feet and ran to the window. She let out an enormous sigh. "It's Mrs. DuVane," she said.

"My goodness," exclaimed Mrs. Sherman. "I didn't expect — oh, lord, right in the middle of dinner . . ."

The Shermans left the table and opened the front door.

From out of her expensive car, which was scrubbed shiny and clean, slid Mrs. DuVane, a large box in her hands. "Hello!" she called. "I'm sorry to come over unannounced, but I wanted to be sure to see Tobias."

"Mommy, Mrs. DuVane has a big present with her. And it's for *Tobias*," said Mae enviously.

Mrs. Sherman patted her daughter's back, then greeted their visitor.

"Oh, you're having dinner," said Mrs. DuVane as she stepped inside. "Well, I won't stay but a minute. It's just that I realized Tobias was going to take off tomorrow and, well, Tobias, I wanted you to have this before you left." She held out the box, which was wrapped in yellow paper and tied with blue ribbon.

"Leavitt's school colors," said Tobias appreciatively as he accepted the package.

"Open it, open it!" cried Mae. She began to jump up and down, then said, "Can *I* open it?"

Tobias smiled and handed the present to Mae. She ripped off the paper, then stared at the box inside. "What is it?" she asked.

Tobias stared. "It's a laptop computer."

"Every student needs his own laptop these days," said Mrs. DuVane.

"Wow. I was going to get a secondhand one next week," said Tobias, "but this . . . this is great. Thank you. I can't believe it."

"You're very welcome. You deserve it. I know that choosing to go to college wasn't easy, and I'm proud of you." Mrs. DuVane looked at the plates of spaghetti on the table, the flickering candles. "I don't want to interrupt your dinner any longer," she said. "I'll be on my way. Stay in touch, Tobias, okay?"

"Now I can send you e-mails," replied Tobias.

Mrs. DuVane held out her hand, but Tobias ignored it and gave her a hug. "I really —"

Mrs. DuVane put her hand on the doorknob. "Not necessary to say anything," she told him. "Good luck!"

And then she was gone.


Later that evening, Nikki took her basket from its hiding place behind the couch. She climbed the stairs to the second floor, stood in Tobias's doorway — and drew in a sharp breath. "Tobias! Your room is almost bare." She looked at the naked bookshelves, the stripped walls, the nightstand empty of everything except an alarm clock.

"Well . . ." he said.

Nikki swallowed a lump in her throat and held out the basket. "This is for you," she said. "It's, um, a good-bye basket. I know it's silly . . ."

Tobias set the basket on his bed. "No, it's great," he said, looking through the items Nikki had selected. "Yellow and blue soap. Very cool. Chocolates. Did Olivia's mother make these?"

Nikki nodded. "And in that," she said, indicating a small plastic picture frame, "you can put a photo of *moi*."

Tobias laughed. But then his smile faded and he said, "You know what I thought when we heard Mrs. DuVane coming up our drive? I mean, before we knew it was Mrs. DuVane?"

"I think so. The same thing I thought — that it was Dad. Which would have been very ironic."

"And scary. Nikki, when I'm gone, you and Mom and Mae are going to be —"

"I know," Nikki interrupted him. "We're going to be all alone out here. But we'll be fine. Really. Mom is . . . Mom. A grown-up. And I'm almost a grown-up."

"That's true."

"Look, we pay our bills now, so the phone always works and, I don't know. Anyway, you can't take care of us forever."

Tobias looked out his window and said nothing.

The next morning he was up early, and by the time Nikki awoke, Tobias's car was loaded, he had eaten breakfast, and he was ready to go.

"So soon?" asked Nikki. She was standing on the front porch in her nightgown, yawning, a sleepy Mae at her side.

"Classes start on Tuesday and I have a lot to do before then."

Mrs. Sherman emerged from the house, dressed for work, a mug of coffee in her hand. She smiled at Tobias. "The first one in this family to go to college," she said. "I'm awfully proud of you."

Tobias hugged his mother and Nikki and swung Mae into the air. "Remember, Mae is in charge while I'm gone," he said. "So Mom, Nikki, be sure to do what she says."

Mae laughed. "I'll write you letters. And you write back, Tobias, but not in cursive, okay? I can't read cursive yet."

"Promise."

Tobias walked to his car but hesitated before climbing into the driver's seat.

Nikki ran to him and gave him a little shove. "Go," she said. "It's time for you to go."

And with that, Tobias slid behind the wheel, pulled the door shut, started the engine, and nosed the car around until it pointed down the Shermans' lane.

"Good-bye!" called Nikki and Mae and their mother.

Tobias honked his horn once.

Nikki watched her brother until all she could see was a small cloud of dust where the lane met the county road.

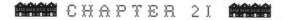

# CHAPTER 21

# Happy Nelson Day

"I wonder how it feels to have an actual *day* named for you," said Ruby. "I'll bet it's better than having a constellation or a sandwich named for you. Today people will go around saying 'Happy Nelson Day!' just like people say 'Happy Halloween!' or 'Happy Thanksgiving!'" She paused and looked at Min and Flora, who were walking on either side of her down Aiken Avenue. "Do you want to know a secret?" She lowered her voice to a whisper. "I kind of wish there was a Ruby Day."

Flora began to laugh, then stopped herself. "I guess it would be exciting to have your very own day."

"The only sad thing," Ruby went on, "is that today is almost the last day of summer vacation."

"It *is* the last day for me," said Flora. "Tomorrow

Nikki and Olivia and I go to the central school for orientation."

"Remember the *first* day of vacation?" said Ruby.

"Yup," replied Flora. "The phoebe babies hadn't hatched yet. And now they're grown and gone."

"The diner hadn't burned down," said Ruby. "And I hadn't met Hilary Nelson."

"Your book club hadn't started," said Min.

"I wasn't a Turbo Tapper," said Ruby.

"It seemed like the summer was going to go on and on forever," added Flora, "and then it went by in a blur."

"Vacations always do that," Ruby said, and sighed.

"But you still have one more day," Min started to say.

"Two for me," interrupted Ruby.

"Okay, one or two," Min amended. "So you might as well enjoy Nelson Day."

They had turned onto Dodds Lane by then and reached the corner of Main Street. "Hey!" exclaimed Ruby. "Look!"

Strung across Main Street was an enormous red banner with black letters reading CAMDEN FALLS CELEBRATES NELSON DAY!

"That is SO cool," said Ruby, and Flora knew full well that her sister was imagining a sign that read CAMDEN FALLS CELEBRATES RUBY DAY!

"Wow, just look at everything," said Flora, her gaze sweeping up and down the street. "It's kind of like the three hundred and fiftieth birthday celebration."

"Oh, it is," agreed Ruby. "The street is closed off again. Look, there are the sidewalk sales." Ruby felt in her pocket for her change purse. She had saved sixteen dollars to spend on Nelson Day. "Is Needle and Thread going to have a sidewalk sale?"

"Of course," said Min. "Nearly every store is."

"I hope the Nelsons get lots and lots of money," said Ruby.

"Hey," said Flora, "you can get your face painted, Ruby."

"And there's Bud. I'm going to have a hot dog for lunch."

"You girls can spend as much time at the street fair as you want," said Min. "Just check in with me at the store once an hour, okay?" Ruby and Flora nodded. "Are Olivia and Nikki going to meet you?"

"At eleven," said Flora.

Ruby and Flora spent half an hour wandering along the west side of Main Street.

"I think I might need some new things for school," said Flora.

"Clothes?" asked Ruby. "Talk to Min. You might find something on sale today. And Min would appreciate it if you saved her some money."

"Actually, I was thinking about, you know, jewelry and hair clips and stuff like that."

"Oh. You need to accessorize," said Ruby. "Min might not pay for those things."

"I know. Come on. Let's look at Bubble Gum's sale. Olivia and Nikki can help me make decisions later."

"What about me? I'm . . ." Ruby hesitated, "pretty accessorable."

Flora smiled. "I know you are."

"How much money do you have?"

"Almost twenty-five dollars."

"Sweet."

Outside Bubble Gum, Ruby and Flora examined the trays and trays of plastic jewelry, hair scrunchies, sunglasses, and barrettes.

"Hey, look!" said Ruby. "Pink cell phone cases. And they glitter."

"For your nonexistent cell phone," replied Flora.

"I'm going to buy these," said Ruby, holding out a pair of tie-dyed socks with peace symbols embroidered on the ankles.

"Very Woodstock," said Flora.

"And I'm going to get this necklace with the beaded peace symbol on it. Hey! I can buy the socks *and* the necklace for six dollars. That's a bargain."

"Hi, you guys!"

Ruby looked up to find Nikki and Olivia making

their way through the crowd that was forming on Main Street. "Hi!" she cried. "We're shopping for school stuff."

"Oh, good," said Olivia. "I need notebooks and pens. Let's see what's on sale at the art supply store."

"And I promised Mae I'd get her new markers," said Nikki.

Ruby, Flora, Olivia, and Nikki spent the next hour going from store to store, looking at jeans and jewelry, notebooks and necklaces.

"Isn't it funny," said Ruby, "how much more fun it is to shop outside than inside? Just like it's more fun to eat outside than inside?"

At the end of the hour, Flora said, "We have to check in with Min now. We might as well leave our bags at Needle and Thread."

"And then let's get something to eat," said Ruby.

Their purchases safely stowed behind the counter at Needle and Thread, Olivia said, "I know what we should get — ice cream."

"Now?" said Nikki. "We haven't even eaten lunch yet."

"Who cares? Today is Nelson Day," replied Ruby. "If today was Ruby Day, I would declare that people could *only* eat ice cream. All day long. Ice-cream cones and ice-cream sundaes and ice-cream sodas and —"

"Okay, we get it," said Flora.

The girls bought Popsicles from the Good Humor

truck that was parked outside Verbeyst's Cleaners and walked along Main Street again, licking vanilla ice cream as it dripped in the morning sun. They saw the Morris kids getting their faces painted. "I'm a kitty cat!" Alyssa called to them. They waved to Mr. Pennington, who was talking to Sonny outside of Time and Again. They saw Aunt Allie sitting in the window of Frank's Beans with a cup of coffee. At last Flora said, "Let's see what's going on in the square." So they crossed Main Street and threaded their way through the knots of shoppers.

In the town square, Ruby approached a kiosk. "Well, look at that," she said, pointing to a sign featuring a cheerful red bar stool. "If we had enough money, we could buy a stool for the Marquis Diner and have it named after us. The stool, I mean. Darn. I don't have nearly enough for that. There isn't a Ruby anything yet. No stool or day or sandwich or constellation. Nothing." She looked at Flora and her friends. "But one day there will be."

"Well, anyway," said Nikki, "buying stools for the diner is a really good idea. I wonder who thought that up. I'll bet tons of money will be raised for the Nelsons today, and that everything will turn out okay for them and they'll be able to stay in Camden Falls after all. Olivia, what's the matter?"

Olivia hadn't been paying attention to Ruby or Nikki. She was staring at a sign behind the kiosk. Ruby now looked over her shoulder and saw a painting of a pink-and-green hot air balloon next to the words BALLOON RIDES: FIFTY DOLLARS. "Olivia?" she said.

Olivia shook her head. "Nothing. I just . . . wow. Fifty dollars."

"Would you actually go up in one of those things?" asked Nikki.

"Well, wouldn't it be fun to see Camden Falls from way up high? You might float over your own house. You'd see Aiken Avenue. And Main Street! You'd look down and there would be the roofs of all the stores. And everyone would be tiny. And then you'd keep on floating, and you'd float out of town and out over the countryside. Now *that* would be a Saturday adventure."

The rest of the afternoon passed in a slow but delicious fashion, and before Ruby knew it, the store owners on Main Street were bringing in their tables, and the shoppers began walking toward the town square. Ruby and her friends split up. Nikki met her mother and Mae, Olivia found her parents and her brothers as they were closing Sincerely Yours, and Ruby and Flora joined Min just as she and Gigi were locking the door of Needle and Thread.

"We'll have supper on the square," said Min cheerfully. "Are you girls hungry or did you have a lot of snacks this afternoon?"

"Hungry," said Ruby and Flora.

At the town square, anyone celebrating Nelson Day dropped five dollars in a large canister and was handed a coupon for a free hot dog or hamburger. Min, Ruby, and Flora, clutching their coupons, wandered the green and greeted their friends and neighbors while in the background the band from the high school played Gershwin tunes and jazz numbers and old rock-and-roll songs that made Min smile.

As dusk was beginning to fall and Ruby saw the flicker of the first fireflies, the band began to play a march. When it was over, a woman wearing a summer pantsuit climbed the steps to the grandstand and tapped on a microphone.

"That's the mayor!" Ruby exclaimed. "Mayor Howie."

"Welcome, everyone," said the mayor. "Thank you all for participating in Nelson Day. As you know, the profits from today's festivities will be donated to the fund in honor of the Nelson family to help them rebuild the Marquis Diner and their home. Over the next few days, the stores that participated in the sidewalk sale will calculate the sum of their donations. But I can tell you right now that the money from the sale of the stools today, from the collection canisters that were set out several weeks ago, and from this evening's donations here on the square total just over twelve thousand dollars."

A cheer rose from the crowd, and Ruby put her fingers in her mouth and let out a whistle.

"And to present that check to the Nelsons," the mayor continued, "I'd like to call to the grandstand Ruby Jane Northrop, who came up with the idea for Nelson Day."

Ruby gasped. She looked at Min, and then she ran to the grandstand and clattered up the steps. Mayor Howie shook Ruby's hand and indicated a giant cardboard check made out to the Nelsons on which someone had written the words TWELVE THOUSAND AND TWENTY-FIVE DOLLARS with a fat black marker. "Now," said the mayor, "I'd like to ask the Nelsons to join us."

While the Nelsons made their way to the grandstand, Ruby grinned at her audience and waved to various friends and relatives. "Ruby," said Mayor Howie when the Nelsons had gathered, "would you do the honors, please?"

The giant check was handed to Ruby then, and she handed it to Mrs. Nelson. Mr. Nelson started to say something to the crowd but had to wait until the cheering and clapping stopped. Finally, he held up his hands, and when the square was quiet, he said, "My family and I moved here to escape the city and to settle into a smaller community. When the fire destroyed our diner, we thought we had lost that chance. Tonight, thanks to all of you, we know we'll be able to finish rebuilding and stay here after all. We've been embraced by Camden Falls, and we want to thank you for your generosity, your support, and most important, for your friendship."

The crowd began to applaud again, and Ruby beamed a movie-star smile as the Nelsons hugged one another and the fireflies twinkled and the moon rose over Main Street.

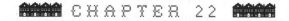 

# CHAPTER 22

# *September*

Camden Falls, Massachusetts, has a different face every day of the year. This is Camden Falls on the evening of Labor Day, which is the first day of September. The Nelson Day festivities are over and Main Street is quiet. The cleaning crew has come through and swept up the candy wrappers and sales receipts, and the sparrows have enjoyed bits of popcorn and the ends of hot dog buns. The lampposts, still twined with gold lights, glow brightly in the dark, and so do the store windows. There's the window of Needle and Thread, now featuring back-to-school clothes made by Min and Gigi and Flora. There's the window of Time and Again, designed by Sonny Sutphin: The rows of books arranged in it have been chosen as Fall Book Club Picks. In the window of Frank's Beans is a sign introducing Pumpkin Spice Chai.

Take a walk through town to a little one-story house in front of which a FOR RENT sign recently stood.

"Pretty soon we can put the sign up again," says Hilary Nelson with satisfaction. "We won't have to live here much longer. We can move back to Main Street."

"We are very, very lucky," says her father.

The Nelsons, all four of them, are sitting in the living room of their rented house. The oversize cardboard check leans against the wall next to the couch.

"We have good friends here," says her mother.

"It's funny how a friend can be someone you never met," remarks Hilary.

In a somewhat larger but even shabbier house on the outskirts of town, Nikki and Mae Sherman and their mother sit at the table in their kitchen. On the floor next to Mae, Paw-Paw is chowing down a bowl of dog food.

"Poor Paw-Paw. He had to eat late tonight," says Mae. "And we got hamburgers, but he only got . . . whatever that stuff is." She leans over to examine the contents of his dish.

"Well, he seems to like it," says Nikki, but her attention is not really on her little sister or on Paw-Paw. She's listening for the sound of cars on the road, and her eyes are trained out the window on the drive to their house. She suspects that her mother is watchful, too. But Mae and Paw-Paw are oblivious to nighttime dangers, and Nikki is grateful for that.

Back in town, lights begin to blink off here and there. In the Morrises' home on the left end of the Row Houses, the light goes off in Alyssa's room. Alyssa, five years old, lies in bed thinking about school. "Kindy garden," she says to herself. "Flower garden, vegetable garden, kindy garden." In three days she will begin kindergarten, and at long last she'll be able to walk to Camden Falls Elementary with her sister and brothers.

In a little plot of land behind the fourth Row House from the right are, somewhat to the surprise of Olivia, Ruby, Nikki, and Flora, flourishing plants that still yield squash, green peppers, eggplants, tomatoes, and more. The moon shines down on the garden, but the only pair of eyes that notices it belongs to Sweetie, Mr. Willet's cat, who has been prowling behind the Row Houses ever since he slipped out the back door, unseen by Mr. Willet, whose mind is on other things.

Inside the Walters' house, Olivia is lying on her bed. She has come up with a new project for herself: She has decided to read all the other books by the authors of the secret book club selections. She decides to start with the books by Elizabeth Enright, who wrote *The Saturdays*, so propped against her knees is a copy of *Thimble Summer*. Olivia is happy to lose herself in a new story, something to yank her mind from thoughts of tomorrow's orientation at the central school.

Three houses away, Bill Willet stands on his front

stoop and looks across his yard to the object that was pounded into the lawn late in the afternoon. Mr. Willet was surprised to learn that the real estate agent worked on Labor Day and now doesn't know whether to be pleased or dismayed by the sight of the FOR SALE sign. He wants to be closer to Mary Lou, but this has been his home for a long, long time. He thinks of the faces of his neighbors as they walked home from the Nelson Day festivities earlier. No one was surprised by the sign, but everyone felt a pang of sadness, the way Olivia felt when she thought over her years at the elementary school, or Mrs. Morris felt when she looked at Alyssa's baby clothes.

"I can't imagine the Row Houses without the Willets," Mr. Fong had said as he and his wife, baby Grace in front of them in her stroller, paused to consider the sign.

"I wonder who'll buy his house," Ruby had said a few minutes later. "We'll have new neighbors."

"The last time we had new neighbors," Min had replied, "was when the Fongs moved here."

Now the Row Houses are quiet. The Morrises have settled in for the night, and so have the Edwardses, the Walters, and Dr. Malone and Margaret. Lydia Malone is out with friends but has a ten o'clock curfew so should be home soon. The Fongs are singing Grace to sleep in her room. Mr. Willet takes one more look at the sign before closing and locking his front door. He hears Sweetie meowing at the back door and opens it gratefully. Sweetie shouldn't be out at night.

One house in the row is dark. Mr. Pennington hasn't come home yet. He's sitting in the living room of Min Read's house. Upstairs, Flora and Ruby are in their bedrooms, neither asleep. Flora is looking through the items she bought at the sidewalk sale and planning her outfit for orientation. Ruby is writing up a list of musicals that feature children, specifically children her age, and planning to present it to someone at the community center. It is her dream to be featured in a musical before she turns twelve.

Downstairs, Min and Rudy Pennington sit side by side on the couch, each wondering what the autumn will bring. They are sitting in silence, but they are very, very happy. Rudy Pennington reaches for Min's hand and covers it gently, and Min smiles into his face.

Hello!

Welcome to the Main Street book club! On the following pages, you'll find a favorite crafting activity of mine, some questions about the series for you to talk about with your friends, and a few recipes—all of which are sure to make your event a hit!

I've been a member of a book club since 2001, and over the years the eight or so women in my club have become close friends—made even closer by the shared experience of reading so many books together. Talking about the most recent book when we go out to dinner once a month is something we look forward to during the weeks between. Over the years we've read fiction, nonfiction, short stories, and biographies, and in reading such a variety of books we've learned a great deal, not only about ourselves, but also about the world around us. Plus, we've had a lot of fun!

So...spend some time on Main Street with Ruby, Flora, Olivia, and Nikki, and do what's most important—have fun!

Sincerely,

Ann M. Martin

Ann M. Martin.

P.S. If you're looking for more recipes, crafting tips, and activities for your event, visit www.scholastic.com/mainstreet!

**SCHOLASTIC**

# Preparing for Your Main Street Book Club!

## 2 weeks ahead:
• Choose a Main Street book to discuss at your event.
• Send an e-mail or printed invitation asking friends to join.

## 1–2 weeks ahead:
• Choose a meeting place (for example, your living room).
• Decide if and how you want to decorate the room.

## 3–4 days ahead:
• Buy snacks and drinks, or buy ingredients you'll need to make them yourself.
• Design your own Main Street—either your own town or Ruby and Flora's town–by decorating your meeting place with handmade store signs, window displays, etc.
• Remind your friends to bring their book to the event. It's much easier to talk about a book when it's right in front of you.

## 1–2 days before:
• Prepare treats (remember, if treats are frozen popsicles, you'll need more time to allow for freezing).

## 1 hour before:
• Set out treats, drinks, and whatever else you'll be snacking on.
• Put pillows or chairs in a circle.
• Wait for your friends to arrive, and have fun!

# Fun No-Bake Recipes
## to Enjoy with Your Friends and Family!

### Rainbow Krispies Treats

Ingredients:

- 3 tablespoons butter
- 1 10 oz. package regular marshmallows (About 40) or 4 cups mini marshmallows
- 6 cups puffed rice cereal
- Rainbow sprinkles

Directions:

1. In large microwave-safe bowl, heat margarine and marshmallows at HIGH for 3 minutes, stirring after 2 minutes until smooth.
2. Add puffed rice cereal. Stir until well coated.
3. Using buttered spatula or waxed paper, press mixture evenly into a brownie pan coated with butter or cooking spray.
4. Sprinkle the top of the mixture with rainbow sprinkles.
5. Cut when cool.

Makes 12 to 16 servings.

# No-Bake Chocolate Refrigerator Cake

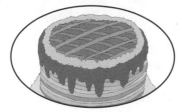

**Ingredients:**
- 1 pint heavy whipping cream
- ¼ cup chocolate syrup
- 1 package graham crackers

**Directions:**
1. Chill bowl and beaters for ½ hour in freezer.
2. Pour whipping cream into chilled bowl and whip on HIGH with beater until cream forms stiff peaks.
3. Add small amount of chocolate syrup to taste until a rich chocolate cream is obtained.
4. In a glass 12- x 8-inch pan, add one layer of graham crackers, then ½ inch layer of chocolate cream. Repeat until pan is full.
5. Chill at least 3 hours before cutting into servings.

Makes 12 servings.

# Make Your Own Yarn Vase!

**Materials:**
- Glass bottle
- Yarn scraps
- Craft glue
- Toothpick

**Instructions:**
1. Cover about one inch of the lower portion of the glass bottle with glue.
2. Wind the yarn around the bottle, tight enough to secure the yarn. (You can use different colors of yarn to make stripes on your vase.)
3. When the glued area is completely covered with yarn, push the rows of yarn closer together.
4. Tuck in the beginning of the yarn with a toothpick, add a little more glue there, and press down for one minute. Don't worry if the glue looks messy. It will dry later!
5. Repeat steps 1–4 until the whole bottle is covered with yarn.
6. Put some pretty flowers in the vase and enjoy!

Modified from http://www.craftown.com/kids/kc10.htm

# Main Street Book Club Discussion Questions

1. By the end of *Main Street #1: Welcome to Camden Falls*, Flora and Ruby have started to adjust to Camden Falls. What changes and growth have you seen in them? Have their relationships with other characters changed? How have the personalities or attitudes changed?

2. In *Main Street #2: Needle and Thread,* Ruby stars in a play about witchcraft in N England in the 1600s called, "The Witches of Camden Falls." What do you know about your hometown's history? Do research with a friend to learn more

3. In *Main Street #3: 'Tis the Season,* the girls decide to take on a project for the Helping Hands charity of Camden Falls by making teddy bears. There are so many important charities in the world. What causes are important to you? Take the time to research different ways to contribute to the causes you care about. How do people contribute their money, their clothing, or their time as volunteer

4. In *Main Street #4: Best Friends,* Flora, Olivia, Nikki, and Annika learn the importance of keeping old friends while making new ones, by talking through their issues together. What are some lessons you have learned from your friends?

5. Who is your favorite Main Street character and why? In what ways do the Ma Street characters remind you of yourself or your friends?

6. What are some activities you do with your best friends? What favorite memor do you share with your best friend?

7. If you could choose one store on Main Street to work at, which store would it b